WHATEVER

WHATEVER
Copyright © 2013 Ann Walsh

RONSDALE PRESS
3350 West 21st Avenue, Vancouver, B.C., Canada V6S 1G7
www.ronsdalepress.com

Typesetting: Julie Cochrane, in Minion 12 pt on 16
Cover Art & Design: Nancy de Brouwer, Massive Graphic Design
Paper: Ancient Forest Friendly "Silva" (FSC)—100% post-consumer waste,
    totally chlorine-free and acid-free

Ronsdale Press wishes to thank the following for their support of its
publishing program: the Canada Council for the Arts, the Government of
Canada through the Canada Book Fund, the British Columbia Arts Council
and the Province of British Columbia through the British Columbia Book
Publishing Tax Credit program.

Library and Archives Canada Cataloguing in Publication

Walsh, Ann, 1942–, author
    Whatever / Ann Walsh.

Issued in print and electronic formats
ISBN 978-1-55380-259-4 (print)
ISBN 978-1-55380-260-0 (ebook) / ISBN 978-1-55380-261-7 (pdf)

    I. Title.

PS8595.A585W43 2013   jC813'.54   C2013-903157-X
                                        C2013-903158-8

At Ronsdale Press we are committed to protecting the environment. To this
end we are working with Canopy (formerly Markets Initiative) and printers
to phase out our use of paper produced from ancient forests. This book is one
step towards that goal.

Printed in Canada by Marquis Printing, Quebec

*This book is dedicated to
the volunteers of Restorative
Justice programs*

ACKNOWLEDGEMENTS

Thank you to Sandra Hawkins, who first introduced me to Restorative Justice; Rod Hawkins, Crown Counsel, Williams Lake, BC, (ret.) and Judy Ross and Nola Crocker of The Center for Epilepsy and Seizure Education British Columbia for their expert advice; Bev Cook for her astute weekly critiques; my fellow writers and friends (Kathleen Cook Waldron, Ainslie Manson, Becky Citra, Heid Redl and Verena Berger) for listening to draft after draft of the manuscript in progress, and to Ron and Veronica Hatch for having faith in the book and adding it to the Ronsdale Press list.

If readers have questions about Restorative Justice or the Canadian criminal law, please check out thelegalbeagle.ca. The website is hosted by a retired Crown Counsel and a Restorative Justice practitioner. Information about epilepsy is available from The Centre for Epilepsy www.epilepsy.cc

This story and all characters are fictional. All references to Restorative Justice (RJ) circles are based on the RCMP model for Community Justice Forums.

Chapter One

THE SOUND OF THE ALARM pulsed against the walls, and echoed back so loud it filled my head as well as the hospital corridor. I ran for the stairs, no way I was going to take the elevator. Down them, two at a time, my heart pounding in my chest, my feet pounding on the steps, my head pounding as if it were about to explode. One floor, another, another. Six, five, four. Between the third and second floors, I bumped into a woman who was inching down the steps, clutching the railing. She yelped, but I didn't turn around—kept moving as fast as I could.

When I reached the main floor, there was chaos. Nurses flew by me, charts in hand, ushering flocks of hobbling, a good job of that. I should never have climbed into the car with her.

After the director's call, it took me half an hour to reach home. I had left my jacket in Mom's car, and the sunny September day had turned cold and cloudy, but I walked slowly anyway, ignoring my freezing fingers. My phone buzzed once, then twice more. Mom. I ignored it. It buzzed again. Dad. I ignored him, too.

When I got home, it was late, after five. Dad was home, early for him, and there was a policewoman in our living room.

"We've been waiting for you, young lady," said the constable. "Sit down."

"Oh, Darrah!" said Mom. "Oh, Darrah, oh, Darrah, oh . . ."

◆ ◆ ◆

At first I denied it. "Of course I didn't pull the fire alarm. Why would I?" There had been no one in the hallway to see me. As mad as I had been, I'd still had sense enough to look around.

The constable grinned. "Ever hear of security cameras, miss? Hospitals are full of them."

"Whatever." I shrugged. "So what? It's not a crime."

"Actually, it is. You have violated Section 437 of the Criminal Code of Canada."

Mom gasped. "What's that?"

"Darrah is guilty of 'willfully, without reasonable cause, by outcry, ringing bells, using a fire alarm, telephone or tele-graph, or in any other manner making or circulating or caus-ing to be made or circulated an alarm of fire ...'" the con-stable itemized, reading from her notebook. "Section 437."

I shrugged. "Whatever. It's no big deal."

"It's against the law to shout 'fire'—or pull a fire alarm—when there isn't any danger. Just as much as stealing or mur-der is against the law. It's a very big deal."

"But I'm not a criminal."

"You are now." The constable's face was serious.

"Why did you ... oh, Darrah ..." Mom again, crying harder.

"I don't know. I guess I was upset." My voice was thin, my throat seemed to have tightened so much I could barely get words out.

"Upset? Please explain." The constable poised a pencil over her notebook. The constable was short and had dark, curly hair. Her uniform fit perfectly, and she had a dimple on her cheek. But even though she was tiny and cute, she scared me.

"Mom promised I could audition, said she'd take me, then she wouldn't drop me at the theatre."

"But, Darrah, Andrew was ..."

"Mom, the doctors told you not to take him to the hospital every time he has a seizure. They taught you how to look after him. You could have—"

"Your mother was worried about your brother."

"Sure, Dad. Like always."

"Tell me exactly what happened. For the report."

"Report? What for? Will it be in the newspaper?" Dad looked horrified.

"This is for the official police report, sir, but it might be mentioned in the paper. No names will be released if it does appear, because Darrah's a youth. But she will be charged and will have to appear before a judge."

"I'm not a 'youth.'"

"In the eyes of the law you are, miss. In criminal law anyone under the age of eighteen is considered a youth."

Criminal law? Judge? Could I go to jail? "I'm sorry, I didn't know..."

"Sorry isn't enough, miss. Do you know someone was hurt when you pulled that alarm?"

"Hurt?" I thought about flapping hospital gowns and crying babies. Maybe someone flapped themselves into a heart attack? "How..."

"When the alarm went off it startled an elderly woman on the stairs. She missed a step and fell. Broke her leg and possibly sprained her arm. She says someone went past her, running, and bumped into her. Was it you?"

A dim memory of a yelp on the stairwell. "Me?"

"Please," begged Mom, "is there any way to settle this without Darrah going to court?"

Dad added his plea. "Can we pay for anything, do anything to keep this from becoming public knowledge? My employers..."

The constable looked at my parents, and shook her head. "No, sir, ma'am, this is a serious offense. There is no way for your daughter to avoid consequences."

"I didn't mean for anyone to get hurt."

"You're lucky it was just one person who was hurt," said the constable. "It only took a few minutes for the hospital staff to realize it was a false alarm, so they didn't have to evacuate a patient in the middle of open-heart surgery or the really sick people who couldn't be moved without risking their lives."

"I'm sorry, I'm really sorry. I didn't mean to . . ." I yammered like an idiot, then I burst into tears. "I didn't mean for anyone to get hurt. I didn't think."

"Oh, Darrah, oh, Darrah," said Mom, but she moved closer to me and put her arm around me.

The constable looked at us—me and Mom weeping, Dad all but on his knees begging her to make this go away. She thought for a moment, wrote something in her notebook, closed it and was silent for a while longer.

"At first I didn't think you would be a good candidate for the program, Darrah, but you now seem genuinely sorry for what you did. So I will suggest an alternative to you and your family. There is a way that you can make amends without going to court, which could easily happen."

"How?" Mom, Dad and I all spoke at once.

"It depends in part on Mrs. Johnson, the woman who was hurt. If she's agreeable, I will recommend that you go through the Restorative Justice program instead of appearing in court."

"Darrah'll do it!"

"That's up to your daughter, Mr. Patrick. Not you."

My choice? I thought for a moment. "What will I have to do?"

"First, you have to take full responsibility for your actions."

"Like a confession? I already did. I said I was sorry."

"During the Restorative Justice circle you must do it publicly, in front of others."

"Others?" Dad was nervous again. "Who else will be there?"

"Who do I have to say it in front of?"

"A representative of the hospital, Mrs. Johnson, your parents and perhaps the principal or counsellor from your school."

"I can't do that."

"It's hard, but that's what you'll have to do."

"Can't I phone everyone and tell them I'm sorry?"

Dad nodded in agreement, he liked my idea.

"No, the circle is a necessary part of the community justice process. You, the offender, and the people you have harmed, the victims, will sit in a circle and face each other."

"Can we turn the lights off? So I don't have to see them?" And they won't see me either, I thought.

The constable smiled. "I don't think that's ever been done, but you can request it."

"Then what happens? What else does Darrah have to do?" Mom pulled me closer.

"She will have to explain what she did and why. Apologize to those affected by her actions. Then everyone discusses what her sanctions will be."

"Sanctions?" I didn't like the sound of that word. "Like how much time I have to spend in jail? Or in one of those juvie places?"

"A circle doesn't administer that type of punishment, Darrah. Sanctions are other ways for you to pay back society for the harm you have done."

"What other ways?"

The constable's radio crackled, she bent her head to her shoulder where it was clipped and spoke softly into it. "Sorry, I've got to leave. Here's my card. Let me know if you and your parents want to go the Restorative Justice route and I'll see if a facilitator can be found for your file."

Mom grabbed the card and looked at it. "Thank you, Constable Markes."

"How soon can we do this circle?" asked my father.

The constable shook her head. "The decision to participate in a RJ sanctioning circle is Darrah's, not yours, sir. Discuss it with her."

"What's a facilitator? When will this circle happen? Do I have to . . ."

But Mom was already ushering the constable out. "Thank you so much for the chance to solve this without going to court. Thank you, Constable, thank you." She was positively oozing gratitude. But she wasn't the one who would have to look a strange woman in the eye and apologize. She wasn't the one who would have to do sanctions, whatever they were. Mom wasn't the one who . . .

"You've been lucky, Darrah." Dad sounded relieved. "Maybe we can keep this in the family. Although I still don't understand why you—"

I shrugged. "Whatever." I pushed past him and went up the stairs to my room. I was going to cry, but I didn't want him to see. I'd already cried in front of my parents once today, I wouldn't do it again.

This wasn't even my fault. It was Mom's. And Andrew's.

Why was I being blamed for something that wasn't my fault?

Chapter Two

EVERYONE LEFT ME alone until dinner. I cried for a bit, then washed my face and gave myself a pep talk. I could handle this circle thing; I'd act contrite and be apologetic about what I'd done. I'd even cry, if I thought it would help. Last year our drama teacher taught us how to cry real tears anytime we wanted to. It was easy to start and easy to stop, so you didn't have to sob until your nose got red and drippy. Maybe I could make everyone so sorry for me that they wouldn't give me any "sanctions" at all.

I was a good actress, I would con everyone. Besides, what could they do to me? The constable said the RJ circle couldn't send me to jail or somewhere else nasty. How hard could this be, anyway?

When I went down for dinner, I began to find out just how hard. Mom and Dad sent Andrew to his room while they talked to me.

"But I'm hungry," he complained, moaning, grabbing his stomach and making a big dramatic deal out of having to wait a few minutes for his food.

Once he left, Dad began, "No matter what sanctions the circle imposes—"

"I haven't decided if I'm going to do the circle."

"You will," said Mom.

"You definitely will," said Dad.

"It's my decision," I reminded them.

"So it is, Darrah, but I think you'll agree that it's a wise choice to go that route. However, regardless of what happens, you've upset your mother on a day when she had all the stress she could handle with Andrew's seizure. You've disappointed us both. Also, your mother and I will have to spend more time on your problem before it can be resolved. You know how pressed for time we both are. So here are your home consequences—"

"Consequences? But, the constable said . . ."

"The constable doesn't control what happens in our home. Your mother and I have decided on several consequences as a result of your actions. First, no cellphone use until after this circle happens. You may take your phone to school, but it is only to be used to call either your mother or me. Once you get home, you may not use it. Close your mouth, we're not done. Second, minimal computer use, for school work only, monitored by me or your mother, until you have completed the sanctions, whatever they will be. We will inform the school that you are not allowed on the school computers except for word processing or research. No games, no Facebook, no whatever else you spend so much time doing online."

"But Dad . . ."

"You're also grounded until the sanctions are completed," added Mom. "No after school activities, no dates—"

"You know I haven't had a date for months."

"Your mother wasn't finished," said my father. "Don't interrupt again."

"No movie dates with friends, no sleepovers, no social activities of any kind," Mom went on. "That's number three."

"What about Halloween? I've already got my costume."

"No Halloween party, unless the sanctions are completed by then."

"That's not fair."

"Perhaps you should think of the old lady who's in hospital because of you. Is that fair? Or of how much stress your actions have caused your mother and me. Is that fair?"

I remembered my pep talk to myself. Act, act, act. Pretend. Get this over with as easily as possible.

"Yes, Father, I mean, no Father," I said meekly and looked down at my folded hands. "I agree."

"You agree! You're kidding, right?"

Andrew hadn't gone far, he had been hiding in the kitchen. The sneak, he'd heard every word.

"None of your business! You're not supposed to be listening, crawl back into your cave."

"Andrew, you were told to go to your room!" said Dad.

Mom shrugged, "Oh, well, I suppose it's all right; he is part of this family. Although he was told to go upstairs."

"He never does what he's supposed to, and you two don't even notice!"

"Andrew," warned Dad.

"Okay, okay, I'm going." He moved out of sight, but I knew he was still listening.

I started to say something else about how Andrew could get away with anything, but changed my mind, shut my mouth and stared meekly at my folded hands. Was there to be a Consequence Number Four?"

Apparently not.

My mother stood up, announcing, "I'm glad that's taken care of. Now let's put this behind us and have a nice family dinner."

Sometimes I wondered what universe Mom lived in. It wasn't this one, that was certain. "A nice family dinner?" Not a chance.

We sat down and opened up the Chinese takeout. Silence. More silence except for the occasional, "Is there more soy sauce?" or "Andrew, put the chopsticks down, you know you'll just make a mess with them." Andrew's always quiet after a seizure, and I didn't have much to say, nor did Dad. Finally Mom began chattering. I guess this was her attempt at a "nice family dinner." Dad didn't respond to her, his eyes kept slipping sideways to me, worried.

I cleared the table, Andrew stacked the dishwasher. "You are both to go to your rooms," said Dad. "Darrah, I'll be up in a minute to move your laptop to the kitchen, where it will stay, understood?"

"Andrew, I'll come with you, dear," said Mom. "You need to take your medication and get ready for bed."

"I don't need to go to bed so early; I slept all afternoon."

"Listen to your mother, Andrew. You know how tired you will be tomorrow. You always are after . . . after . . . go on, upstairs with you." Dad didn't like to say the words "seizure" or "epilepsy." Maybe he thought the disease would go away if he didn't give it a name.

"You can bring your marks up," Mom told me in her cheerful voice, "since now you won't be wasting so much time on that Facebook stuff."

Upstairs, I wrote a quick Facebook post. "Grounded, no phone, no computer, no life. Call me on land line." I added the family number, thought for a minute, then erased the entry instead of hitting "post." I wasn't ready to talk about what had happened.

I watched Dad confiscate my laptop and reluctantly handed over my phone. Once he had gone back downstairs, Andrew stuck his head in my door. "What stupid thing did you do now?"

He had been asleep when the constable was here. He always sleeps after a seizure, so he didn't know what had happened. "I bet it was really dumb. But, no computer, ouch. Hey, if you want me to . . ."

"Shut up. It's none of your business." I almost added, "Anyway, it's your fault," but something made me hold the words back.

"They didn't keep me long in the hospital," said Andrew, assuming I cared. "They told Mom not to bring me back there unless a seizure lasted more than five minutes or I hurt myself or had a whole bunch in a row."

"The doctors told her that last time."

"Oh." Then, "What about rehearsals? You got the part, didn't you? Will they let you off being grounded to go to rehearsals?"

"I . . . I . . . oh, go away." I buried my head on my arms. "Get lost," I said through my sleeve.

"Dar? You crying?"

"Leave me alone!"

I heard Andrew take a few steps into the room and stop. I bit my arm, trying to muffle the sobs that were sneaking up on me.

"Dar?"

"Go away."

He left, shutting the door behind him and I was alone with my tears for the second time that day.

◆ ◆ ◆

Constable Markes was back the next afternoon. I was home from school early as commanded by my parents' Third Consequence, so I answered the door. At the sight of her, my heart sped up and sweat rushed to my underarms. "Uh, hi."

"How you doing, Darrah?" she asked.

"Okay, I guess." I was surprised by her question.

"Really?"

I sighed and told the truth. "No. The whole thing sucks."

"Yup," she said. "But it could suck a lot worse, believe me."

I ushered her into the living room and called Mom. Andrew was home. I saw him hovering in the kitchen. I glared at him and he disappeared, but I knew he was still within earshot.

Once we were seated and the constable had refused a cup of tea or coffee or anything else, and Mom had stopped fluttering around, the constable asked, "Are you willing to participate in the Restorative Justice program, Darrah?"

"She is," said Mom.

"Please, Mrs. Patrick, I've told you, I need to hear Darrah say it. Not you."

I went into my role. "Oh, yes, Constable Markes, and thank you for giving me the opportunity to do this."

She paused for a moment, looked hard at me, then went on. "You will have to sign a form confirming that. I'll go over the questions with you."

"Of course," said Mom, "We're ready."

The official form I had to sign had a blue logo at the top, and a circle of people with their arms raised. I could make out the words "community" and "justice."

"First question, Darrah. 'Do you understand and agree that you are responsible for the following matter, Violation of Section 437 of the Criminal Code of Canada and causing accidental harm to a civilian?'"

Silence. Even Mom had nothing to say this time.

"Darrah?" asked the constable. "Do you understand?"

"Yes," I mumbled.

"Do you admit your responsibility in this matter?"

Silence again.

"Take your time," said Constable Markes. "Make sure you realize that you are admitting your guilt and accepting full responsibility for what you did."

"Um ... I guess so."

"Pardon? I couldn't hear you."

"Yes, I did it, okay? Can we get this over with?" I was almost shouting.

"Darrah, manners!" pleaded Mom.

"It's okay, ma'am, that's the hardest question for most people."

The other questions were easier: "... Do you understand that if you do not participate in the conference, the RCMP can take other action, that any person who considered themselves affected by your actions could attend the circle, that if you ..."

"Hey, can I come too?" Andrew appeared in the living room, interrupting the flow of questions. I knew he'd be listening.

"No way!"

"I don't think it would be appropriate, Andrew," said Mom. Not a word about him sneaking around and eavesdropping.

"But I've been affected because Mom and Dad are upset. So I'm allowed to come and find out what happened, the cop just said so. Right, Constable?"

"I'll leave that decision up to your parents and the facilitator," said Constable Markes. "But it's encouraging that you want to support your sister at the circle."

"Support?" said Andrew. "Oh . . . "

The constable looked at her watch. "Darrah, since you have agreed to all the conditions required by the RJ process, please sign this form."

Mom had to sign, too, because I was still a "youth" in the eyes of the law. Andrew tried to sneak close enough to get a better look at the form, but Constable Markes shook her head at him and he backed off.

"That's it, then," said the constable. "You're lucky, there is a facilitator available to take your file. The facilitators are volunteers, and sometimes they are all busy with other cases. I have some paperwork to do at the station, then I'll send Mrs. Barrett your information. She's a retired teacher, very keen on the RJ process."

She handed Mom a piece of paper. "Here's the information. Call her as soon as you can. She'll need to set up a pre-interview with you and Darrah, and, of course, arrange a time for the circle that suits everyone."

"I'll call her right away," said Mom.

"How long? I mean, how long before the circle happens? Will the sanctions be over by Halloween?"

"Once you get in touch with Mrs. Barrett, she'll do everything she can to make it happen soon. It partly depends on my availability."

"You'll be there?"

"Part of my job. I'm the official RCMP representative for your case so I have to be there. Officers attend circles during working hours, so I have to check my shifts and find out when I'm available."

"You'll be there?" I asked again.

"Wouldn't miss it for anything. Besides, usually the facilitators bring cookies, homemade ones. And juice or pop."

Mom showed the constable out. I sat, stunned. Cookies and constables? Juice and justice? Facilitators? Sanctions? What had I agreed to do?

Chapter Three

MOM CALLED MRS. BARRETT and left a message, and another one, and another one, but we didn't hear from her for almost two weeks. When we did she apologized and explained that she'd been called out of town unexpectedly ("a small family crisis, nothing serious") and had just returned. "There wasn't another facilitator available to take your file," she said. "I'm sorry you had to wait until I got back, but now I'll start the process immediately."

The "process" moved slowly. I sat at home with no phone, no Facebook, nothing to do but read. Andrew watched re-runs of the old *Star Trek* series after school—Mom thought they were good for him, not much violence and people of different types and species getting along with each other. Besides, she said, as he couldn't play soccer anymore, a bit of TV wouldn't hurt.

After the Consequences were laid down and I had nothing else to do, I started to watch with him. I was bored at first, and then the campy shows grabbed me. Andrew printed out information about all three series for me and, as he'd seen most of the episodes already, he kept up a running commentary during the shows. That was how I spent my afternoons, being indoctrinated into the cult of the Trekkies. Some of the costumes in the shows were great; I began to rethink my Halloween vampire outfit.

But it was already early October and Mrs. Barrett hadn't given us a date for the circle yet, so my getting out of the house on Halloween was seeming less and less likely.

Mom and I had to meet with Mrs. Barrett before she could arrange the circle. She explained that this meeting was to make sure we understood how the Restorative Justice process worked. After an hour of her explaining and asking me questions and Mom crying and "Oh, Darrah"-ing, Mrs. Barrett said that she would have a circle date for us as soon as she'd arranged a time with Constable Markes and Mrs. Johnson.

It was almost a week after that meeting when she called to say that everyone else could attend a circle this coming Wednesday night. Would that be convenient for us? Convenient? Did it matter? I had to go through with it, "convenient" or not. I'd waited almost a month for this circle; I wanted to get it over with. All that time with no phone, no Facebook and nothing to do on weekends except sit home and watch more *Star Trek* reruns. I couldn't even remember what a mall looked like, it had been so long since I'd been to one.

I was nervous now that the circle was finally arranged, but I kept reminding myself of my pep talk: I would act sweet, act sorry, act anyway I could to make the whole thing go away quickly.

Andrew protested loudly about having to stay home, but Mrs. Barrett had said it was up to me whether or not he came to the circle. Definitely not, I told him. Every time he asked.

The circle was held in a meeting room in one of the hotels. In the lobby was a sign that said "Restorative Justice – Room 209." I snuck a look around, but no one was in the lobby to see Mom and Dad and I climb into the elevator and wonder where we were going or what we were doing there.

The meeting room was small and stuffy, even though the air conditioner was on. It whined as it blew the smell of stale cigarette smoke around. Apparently this wasn't one of the hotel's smoke-free venues.

Mrs. Barrett was already there, and she greeted us at the door. "I have name tags on your seats. Please sit where I've placed you."

My name tag was right beside hers, Mom was next to me and Dad beside her. Under a couple of the chairs were boxes of tissues. Constable Markes had arrived before us and was seated next to Dad's place. Her name tag lay on the floor in front of her. There was a name I didn't recognize on the next chair. On Mrs. Barrett's other side sat an old lady, a blue cast on her leg, one hand gripping a cane.

"The representative from the hospital had to cancel at the last minute," Mrs. Barrett said, pulling the empty chair away from the circle. "An emergency of some sort. However, both the constable and I have spoken to him, and he told us what he feels would be an appropriate sanction, from the hospital's point of view. I've asked the constable to pass on his ideas."

I sat down, deliberately sitting on my name tag. Everyone knew who I was, why had she bothered with a stupid tag? Mrs. Barrett sat down and pulled her chair closer into the circle. She coughed and started to say something, then suddenly pushed the chair back, got up, turned off the noisy air conditioner, shut the door to the hall and sat back down. After she had pulled her chair in again she said, "Now I think we're ready." She seemed nervous, although I couldn't figure out why. This circle wasn't about her.

Our chairs were so close together I had to be careful not to let my knees bump into hers. All the chairs were close together. Dad had pushed his back a bit so he wasn't rubbing elbows with the constable.

Mrs. Barrett reached under her chair and brought out a clipboard with papers attached to it and said, "We are all here, so let's begin. Welcome, everyone. My name is Mrs.

Barrett and I am the facilitator of tonight's forum. I'm going to begin by introducing everyone and giving their reasons for participating in today's circle."

Around the circle her eyes went, stopping at each chair, saying the person's name and why they were there, introducing us as if this were some sort of stupid classroom game and most of us hadn't already met each other. Next she'd be asking us to name our hobbies and our pets.

The last person to be introduced was the old lady. "This is Mrs. Johnson," Mrs. Barrett said. "She is the one most hurt by what happened."

Yeah, well, that was sort of obvious. The cast gave it away.

Mrs. Barrett went on. "Now that the introductions are over, I will remind you that we are not here to judge Darrah's character. We are here to learn how others have been affected by her actions and to find ways to repair the harm that she has done. Do you all understand this?"

Once more she went around the circle, making eye contact with everyone, making sure she was understood. The chairs were so close together that she could have seen us all nod agreement at once, without making such a big deal about it.

I stared at the floor, trying not to look at Mrs. Johnson. She was wearing glasses, and her eyes seemed huge, magnified by the thick lenses. She wouldn't stop staring at me. I moved further back in my chair, so Mrs. Barrett blocked the old lady's view of me.

Mrs. Barrett read from the papers on her clipboard.

"Darrah, your presence here is voluntary. You are free to leave this circle at any time. However, if you do choose to leave, this matter will be dealt with in a different way."

There was nothing I wanted more than to get up and walk out, away from this stupid circle, away from my parents and Mrs. Barrett and the old woman who was staring at me. Away from the little constable, who somehow looked much taller tonight, even though she was sitting down.

"Darrah, do you understand?"

"She does," answered my mother.

Of course I understood. Mrs. Barrett, when she met with me and Mom last week, had explained it twice. The alternative to being at this circle tonight meant I had to go to court and stand before a judge, just like a murderer or a mugger.

"Darrah?" she asked again. "Do you understand? We need to hear your answer."

Mom elbowed me. "Whatever," I said, under my breath.

Mom poked me harder.

"Yes, of course I understand," I said out loud, remembering how I'd decided to handle this circle. "You explained it very well the other day, Mrs. Barrett, thank you," I said politely.

I understood all right. They could call it a "Restorative Justice Circle" or they could call it a "Community Justice Circle" or they could call it one of the circles of Hell. But no matter what anyone called it, I was on trial.

"You are reminded that the discussions here today are confidential and that we will remain respectful so that we all can feel safe. Everyone will have a chance to speak. Darrah, I understand some of the teachers in your school know of this incident, perhaps some of your friends do, too, but—"

"Everyone knows," said my father. "The news has even reached my co-workers. I thought you said this process would be confidential?"

"Unfortunately, no one can control what the community talks about, Mr. Patrick. Be assured that no information came from either the constable or me."

That didn't help much. Half the town apparently knew what I'd done.

"Darrah has admitted her role in this matter. We will start by asking her to tell us what happened." Mrs. Barrett was reading from the papers on her clipboard again.

I said nothing. I didn't want to say anything. Maybe, if I kept quiet, I could . . .

Mom poked me again. On my other side, Dad folded his arms and grunted a warning. "Darrah," Mrs. Barrett repeated. "Please tell us what happened on that day."

"Does she have to?" That was the old woman. She shifted on the chair, pushing her leg forward. Her right arm was tucked into a sling and she wore old, faded Levis with the right leg cut open along its side, to make room for the cast. Her bare toes were white and stuck out from the end of the cast. They were so white they were almost blue, colour coordinating with both cast and jeans. But her toenails were thick and a gross yellow colour. No colour coordination there. I looked away from her bare foot.

"Yes, Mrs. Johnson, she does have to tell everyone what she

did," said the facilitator. "It's part of the circle process. You and I discussed what would happen tonight."

"I know, I know, you explained. But if the girl's admitted she did it, what's the point? These chairs aren't very comfortable and my toes are cold." She wriggled them, yellow nails and all.

"I apologize, Mrs. Johnson. Would you like me to see if I can find you a pillow."

"Won't help much," she said, shifting her leg again. "It's not just my derrière that hurts. It's my leg, too."

"Can I find a blanket to cover your foot?"

I suspected I wasn't the only one who had noticed the yellow toenails.

"Nope. And let's finish this."

Mrs. Barrett looked down at the papers again. She had told Mom and me that, as a facilitator, she had to follow a script which specified what she was to say, what questions to ask at the circle. The RCMP had designed this script, she said, and all over Canada, wherever another poor person was having to suffer through one of these circles, the same words would be read, the same questions asked. Mrs. Barrett flipped a few pages, but I guess the script didn't tell her what to do when someone complained about a sore butt and cold toes.

"I'm sorry, Mrs. Johnson," she said, looking up. "But we have to hear from everyone. It's required in a Restorative Justice circle."

"Okay, let's do it. Come on, girl, answer the questions so we can finish this and go home."

"It won't take long. Darrah, tell us what happened."

I mumbled to the floor. "I pulled the fire alarm."

"Please tell us why you did that."

"I don't know."

"You said, at our interview, that you were missing an important event because you were at the hospital."

"Yes."

"And? Please tell us more."

I thought for a moment, trying to think of the words that would make everyone sorry for me. "It was Mom's fault. She made me go to the hospital with her. She was speeding, driving dangerously. I told her to slow down, that it wasn't an emergency. Andrew's had lots of seizures since last year when they found out he was sick."

I paused for a moment and thought about how my parents always seemed to be scurrying around like frantic rabbits. They'd been scurrying ever since Andrew's diagnosis—to specialists, to our family doctor, to the clinic in Vancouver, to pharmacies, to support groups for families with epilepsy, to the school to talk to his teachers, to . . .

"Go on."

"Mom made me sit in the back seat and hold Andrew, even though he was strapped in and didn't need holding. She wouldn't listen when I asked her to drop me off near the theatre. She wouldn't even stop the car so I could get out and catch a bus, and . . ."

Oops. These weren't the words of someone who wanted sympathy. I took a deep breath, told myself to settle down.

But when I opened my mouth, what came wasn't what I had planned. "I begged her to stop the car, Andrew was fine, his seizure was over, he was asleep. But she wouldn't listen to me. Then I waited all alone outside the emergency room, and no one told me what was happening, and that snarky nurse wouldn't let me use my phone."

"Go on, Darrah." Everyone was staring at me. I took another deep breath. "Maybe if I'd phoned the director sooner, he would have waited for me instead of giving the blonde my part." I shrugged. "I was hungry, so I went upstairs to get something to eat, but the cafeteria was closed and when I wanted to go back down, the stupid elevator was slow . . ." I stopped again. Again everyone waited. "That was when I pulled the fire alarm."

"What were thinking when you did that?"

"Nothing."

"Nothing?"

"Okay, I was mad, all right? I wasn't thinking. I was missing my audition and Dad walked right by me even when I called to him and . . ."

Dad looked surprised; he hadn't noticed me in the waiting room. He shook his head, "But I had to see how Andrew was—"

"Andrew, Andrew, Andrew, that's all you and Mom have said for months! I might as well not even exist." Once more, this wasn't what I had planned to say. I stopped talking before I could do myself any more damage.

"Please go on," said Mrs. Barrett.

I shook my head. "That's all." I didn't want to say any more than I already had. My great plan of acting contrite and apologetic and getting off with easy sanctions was in ruins.

"Is there something else you'd like to say? To anyone here?"

I shook my head.

"Are you sure?"

"Yes."

She sighed, "All right, Darrah. I'll ask you that question again later." She turned to the old woman. "Mrs. Johnson, please tell us what happened to you when Darrah pulled the fire alarm."

"You know what happened. So does the constable. I told you both."

"Yes, but you need to tell it again, here in the circle."

Mrs. Johnson shrugged, then winced as her arm followed her shoulder's movement. "I fell. Shouldn't have been using the stairs, but the elevator was slow, just like the girl said. Then the alarm sounded, and I figured I'd better get out of there in a hurry so I turned around and started back down. I fell. That's it."

"When you told the constable about the incident, you said that someone bumped into you."

"I was confused. In shock. No one bumped me. I moved too quickly and tripped over my own feet. Wasn't wearing my glasses."

I bit my lip. Why did she say that? I was sure she was the

person I had bumped into as I rushed to get out of the hospital. I hadn't seen her actually fall, but I was moving so fast I
was probably out the door by the time she hit the ground.

Mrs. Barrett turned to the constable. "Did you check the
security tapes for the stairs, Constable?"

"Yes, ma'am. But, right at the point where Mrs. Johnson
fell, there's a blind spot. You can see Darrah heading towards
her, then the cameras don't show anything until the next
landing. Darrah's running so fast she's almost a blur, but you
can tell it's her by what she's wearing."

"Mrs. Johnson, are you sure no one caused you to fall?"
Mrs. Barrett asked again.

The old lady leaned forward, peering around Mrs. Barrett.
She stared right at me as she answered. "I'm sure. I fell, that's
all."

The constable and Mrs. Barrett exchanged glances, then it
was Mrs. Barrett's turn to shrug. It was a small movement,
and she corrected it almost as soon as it began, but I saw it.

"We'll go on then. How did you feel when this happened,
Mrs. Johnson?"

"Besides being in pain and not able to stand up? I was
scared. I didn't know if there really was a fire and I'd be
trapped on the stairs. The alarm was loud, there was shouting, lots of noise. I cried out but knew no one could hear me,
so I lay there until you showed up, young lady." She smiled at
the constable. "I was never so glad to see anyone in my life."

Constable Markes mumbled something about it being her
job, glad to help, and looked at her well polished black shoes.

I could see a red flush moving up to her cheeks.

"How has this affected you, Mrs. Johnson?" Mrs. Barrett was reading from her script again.

The old woman looked at her as if she thought the facilitator were out of her mind. "How has it affected me?" she repeated. "That's rather obvious, isn't it? There's a cast on my leg because it's broken, and a sling on my arm."

"Can you be more specific about how you've been affected by the incident?"

"I guess you want details. Okay, to begin with, I don't get out much. Can't drive. Can't hang out the laundry or dig up the potatoes. Can't carry a cup of tea and a book from the kitchen to my favourite chair in the living room because I need one hand to hold the cane. For a while they had me in a wheelchair and I couldn't push it properly with only one good arm. Kept going in circles."

She stopped, and the room was silent, the kind of silence that makes you think of floating in deep space or standing alone on a glacier. Even Mrs. Barrett didn't interrupt to read something from her script. She waited, like the rest of us. Finally the old lady sighed and went on. "I guess what hurts most is that I didn't get to see my friend in the hospital. He died that afternoon while they were fixing me up. That's why I was there. To say goodbye."

She stopped speaking and again there was that deep, cold silence. Then I burst out, "I didn't mean for anyone to get hurt."

Mom grabbed a tissue from the box under her chair and

dabbed at her eyes. Dad cleared his throat and shifted on his chair.

"Darrah is normally a very responsible girl," he said. "We don't know what got into her that day."

"Thank you, Mr. Patrick. You'll have your turn to speak as soon as Mrs. Johnson has finished. Tell us, Mrs. Johnson, what has been the hardest thing for you since this happened?" Another question from the script.

"Besides not being able to take a shower unless someone wraps my leg in a plastic garbage bag and helps me get in and out? Besides not being able to put the garden to bed for the winter? Besides not being able to sleep because the cast itches? Besides having to perch on a damned plastic throne on top of the toilet seat because I can't bend my knee enough to sit on the regular seat?"

"Uh . . . yes, besides all that." Mrs. Barrett was scanning the facilitator's script again, turning pages furiously.

"What do you think?" asked Mrs. Johnson. "What do you think is the hardest thing for me since this happened? None of it has been fun. So finish up with this circle nonsense and let me go home. I need my 'throne' if you get my drift."

Chapter Four

WE TOOK A SHORT BREAK. When Mrs. Barrett and the old lady were back, it was the constable's turn to speak to the circle.

"Constable Markes, do you have anything to add to Darrah's account of what happened? Is what she told us correct?" asked Mrs. Barrett.

The gun strapped to the constable's waist appeared heavy enough to make her lean sideways. But she sat with her back as straight as the tin soldiers my grandfather used to keep on his bookshelf.

"Yes, ma'am." She pulled out her notebook and began to read. "I was called to the scene in response to the fire alarm. I found Mrs. Johnson in the stairwell and made sure she got medical attention. Then I viewed the security tapes, and one of the nurses was able to identify Darrah Patrick as the person seen breaking the alarm. She further recognized the offender as coming to the hospital with a woman and young boy who had suffered an epileptic fit. The nurse said the offender was disobeying hospital rules by using her cellphone in the emergency waiting area and had shown attitude when she was reprimanded." She paused to take a breath.

"Thank you, Constable."

"I'm not done, ma'am." The constable frowned at Mrs. Barrett.

"Sorry, please go on."

"I obtained the pertinent information from the nurse and, after contacting her parents, proceeded to the offender's home where, in the presence of her parents, she was offered the opportunity to settle this matter out of court through Restorative Justice. Although the offender at first seemed to treat the incident casually, both she and her parents have been most cooperative since. That's all."

"Thank you, Constable."

Attitude? I glared at the constable who wasn't even looking at me. I hadn't shown "attitude" that day; it was that nurse who had. "Didn't you see the signs, young lady?" she had asked, really cold and stuck up. "Go outside if you need to call your boyfriend." As if I had a boyfriend to call.

Mom was talking to the circle, but I hadn't been listening.

She suddenly burst into tears and Mrs. Barrett reached under a chair and pulled out another tissue from the box. She handed it to Mom. "Take your time, Mrs. Patrick."

"I don't know how Darrah could do it, I really don't," Mom sobbed. "The last few months, she's been different. Her grades went down and she spent all summer in her room, on her laptop. Oh, Darrah, oh, Darrah, oh . . ." She put her hand on my shoulder. I tried to shrug it off.

"Mr. Patrick, do you have anything to add?"

"My wife's explained things pretty well. Darrah's a responsible girl, always has been, except maybe not so much lately. I don't know why she did this."

"Thank you all. Unless anyone has anything else to say, we will now discuss what sanctions should be imposed on Darrah so that this matter can be resolved. But before we begin that stage of the circle, I'll ask again. Darrah, is there anyone in this room you would like to say something to?"

I shook my head without looking up. Mom poked me in the ribs again. "Manners," she whispered.

Finally I understood. I took a deep breath, made my eyes go wide and sad. "I'm sorry you got hurt, Mrs. Johnson. I beg you, from the bottom of my heart, please forgive me. I didn't mean to harm you." I was staring at the floor as I said that; I couldn't face the old lady.

"Look at Mrs. Johnson and say that again please, Darrah," said the facilitator.

No way! That was a great speech, but I couldn't do it again, not with a straight face. But I lifted my head and looked at the woman, trying to make my eyes go blurry and sad at the same time, so I couldn't really see her. She stared back through her thick glasses.

"Um ... ah ... I ..." My tongue was thick and my eyes wouldn't stay unfocused. She kept staring at me, waiting. "I'm s ... s ... sorry," I stammered.

Mrs. Johnson nodded at me, but didn't say anything. Mrs. Barrett was still looking at me expectantly. "Anyone else?" she asked.

This was a test. Mrs. Barrett had that same look on her face as Mom does when she asks me one of those trick questions. Like, "When was the last time you did your laundry?" after she'd probably already seen my overflowing laundry hamper, or the stains on my jeans. There was a right answer to Mrs. Barrett's question, and I'd better come up with it fast. What was I supposed to say?

"Oh, Darrah," breathed my mom and began to cry again.

Got it! I turned to her. "I'm sorry Mom. And Dad. I didn't mean to put you through this. I'm so sorry." I was acting again, doing a great job, not really thinking about what I was saying.

"Oh, Darrah," Mom grabbed my hand.

Then, to my surprise, I burst into tears. Real tears, not stage ones. Mrs. Barrett produced another box of tissues and handed it to me. Mom hugged me, and Dad patted me reassuringly on my back.

"I'm really, really sorry, for everything," I said through my tears. "I didn't mean to hurt anyone."

"Thank you, Darrah," said Mrs. Barrett.

"Good," said Mrs. Johnson. "She's said she's sorry, so let's go home." She shifted in her chair and reached for her cane, getting ready to stand up.

"Not yet. The circle isn't finished. Would you like me to take you to the handicapped bathroom again before we proceed, Mrs. Johnson?"

"Don't need to do any more proceeding, far as I'm concerned. The girl apologized. That's good enough for me. Let's wind this up."

I was solidly with Mrs. Johnson on this point. Let's just forget any sanctions and go home. But no one else spoke up to agree.

"We're nearly done. But first, Darrah, have you thought about what you might do to make amends for your actions?"

I stopped crying immediately. The sanctions were how I would pay for my actions. Mrs. Barrett had said that sanctions weren't punishment, and I shouldn't think of them that way. "It's doing whatever you can to make things as right as they can be." She'd asked me to think about what I could do, like community service, something that helped others.

"I thought about writing letters, apologizing."

"Who would you write to?"

"Mrs. Johnson. The hospital, too, I guess."

"The representative from the hospital suggested a letter,"

added the constable. "After he finished talking about the in-convenience and Darrah's irresponsibility and—"

"Thank you, Constable, we don't need to hear anymore. I had a conversation with the same person, and much of what he said about Darrah is judgmental and must not be repeated here.

"What do the rest of you think about Darrah writing two letters of apology as one of her sanctions?"

Everyone nodded.

"All right, that's decided. Mr. and Mrs. Patrick, will one of you take responsibility for making sure Darrah does this and go with her to deliver them in person?"

"I'm sure my wife can find time for that," said Dad. "And I will proofread the letters and make sure they're sincere."

"Is that agreeable to you, Darrah?"

"Can't I mail them?"

"No," said my father, "I think you should deliver them yourself. And apologize in person as well."

Thanks Dad. Thanks for making this harder for me. I glared at him, then nodded and mumbled, "Sure." What choice did I have?

"Good." Once again Mrs. Johnson reached for her cane to get up. Mrs. Barrett pretended not to see her.

"Darrah, at our pre-circle interview, I told you that sanctions often are time spent helping in the community. Have you thought about helping out in the soup kitchen or charity thrift store on the weekends?"

"Last year Darrah was very involved with her school's drama program," said my father. "She often had to rehearse on the weekends. We think it would be good for her to participate again this year."

"I don't understand," said Mrs. Barrett. "I thought Darrah missed her chance to be in the play."

"That wasn't a school play I was auditioning for, that was amateur theatre, real theatre, nothing to do with the school," I said. "I didn't get the part and there won't be another chance to audition for anything until after Christmas. I don't mind weekends."

"Isn't the school doing *A Christmas Carol*?" asked Mom.

"I didn't audition."

My father looked surprised. Then he said, "Andrew will be playing soccer again soon."

My mother's turn to look surprised. None of the doctors had said anything about Andrew going back to soccer, as far as I knew.

"Excuse me?" said Mrs. Barrett, "I'm not sure what your son's soccer has to do with this circle, Mr. Patrick."

"We like to watch his games as a family; I'd prefer it if Darrah could be free on the weekends, so she could come."

"I understand," said Mrs. Barrett. "Perhaps it would be best if we keep your weekends open, Darrah."

"Can I get the sanctions done by Halloween?" I asked.

"It's unlikely," said Mrs. Barrett.

There went my chance of going to the Halloween party. I

was grounded until after the sanctions had been done, my parents' Consequence Number One.

"Then it doesn't matter to me. I'll work in the soup kitchen if I have to," I said.

"I'd rather we found something else she could do," said my mom. "I think there are some . . . some dangerous people who go there. Street people."

"She'd be supervised and quite safe," assured Mrs. Barrett. "But if you don't like the idea, then of course she won't be placed there. These sanctions are your decision, all of you."

"What can she do on weekdays?" asked my father.

Mrs. Barrett was flipping pages again. "Not much. If it were summer, she could help at the community garden or serve lunches at the seniors' centre. But as it's now the middle of October, there won't be any work in the community garden until spring. The seniors' centre closes at three, before Darrah could get there after school."

"I told you, I'll work at the soup kitchen. But not the thrift store." Handling all those old, smelly clothes, ugh.

"Let's see if anyone else has a suggestion. Mrs. Patrick? Do you have any ideas?"

Mom shook her head. "Maybe one of the churches . . ."

Mrs. Barrett shook her head. "I suspect that helping at a church would also involve weekends. I can probably find something else, but I have to do some research to see what's available this time of year."

"Something else?" I didn't like the sound of that, either.

Dad had a suggestion. "Maybe she could bring up her marks?"

"That's up to Darrah, Mr. Patrick, and outside the ability of this circle to enforce. However, I'm sure she will—"

Mrs. Johnson coughed and Mrs. Barrett jumped, "Oh, Mrs. Johnson, I was supposed to ask you for your input right after I asked Darrah. I'm so sorry I skipped you. Do you have a suggestion?"

"I don't need a letter," said the old lady. "She said she was sorry, that's good enough to me. But this sanction thing, I've been thinking. There's a caregiver that comes in and helps me shower and makes sure I have my meals, but I could use help with other chores around my place. Those potatoes have to be dug up before they freeze, and there's other things I can't do right now. Would her giving me a hand fit the rules of this circle?"

Mrs. Barrett nodded, then spoke to my parents. "Mr. and Mrs. Patrick, would you agree to Darrah helping Mrs. Johnson after school for a few hours a week?"

"I don't want—" I began, but Mom's voice was louder.

"That's a good idea."

My father agreed. "Darrah's a very capable person. She could be a lot of help."

"Constable?" asked Mrs. Barrett.

"Works for me," answered the constable.

"Darrah, how do you feel about that?"

I opened my mouth to object, then shut it and took a deep

breath. "I want to make things right," I said. Which didn't really answer the question. I did not want to dig up potatoes, mess around with mud, worms and maybe spiders. Besides, I don't know how to dig up potatoes. I didn't want to do housework, either, but there didn't seem to be much point in disagreeing.

"Good. We now need to discuss how many hours Darrah will spend with Mrs. Johnson."

Mrs. Johnson held out for me working for her every school afternoon until Christmas! "My cast can come off in a few weeks," she said, "but the doctor said my leg will be weak and I have to do exercises and take it easy until the muscles get stronger. I'll need help for a long time."

Mom suggested twenty hours, an hour every school day for a month; Dad said he thought Mrs. Johnson should have help longer, maybe a hundred hours. Mrs. Barrett, as the facilitator, wasn't allowed to suggest anything.

After a time, everyone agreed on fifty hours, two and a half hours every Monday and Wednesday.

Finally, Mrs. Barrett turned to me. "Darrah, do you think this is fair?"

For a moment I didn't say anything. I thought about saying I thought it was completely unfair and I wasn't going to do it. Then I thought about standing in front of a judge and having to go through all of this again and maybe getting a punishment worse than helping with housework. Besides, I was already grounded until the sanctions were over. What else did I have to do after school except do homework and watch more *Star Trek*? I shrugged.

"Whatever . . ." Mom glared at me so I went on, "Whatever you think. I just want to get this over with."

"I will now ask you all if you are satisfied with the agreement we have reached." Mrs. Barrett went around the circle again and solemnly asked everyone. I nodded. Mrs. Johnson said that would be fine; Mom and Dad both looked relieved when they said were they were happy with the sanctions; the constable added that she thought it was satisfactory. Of course she thought it was "satisfactory." She wasn't the one who would have to dig up all those potatoes. She grinned at me, as if she knew exactly what I was thinking.

"Now, I will ask you all to sign this agreement." Mrs. Barrett passed it to me first. At the top was some formal language saying I had participated in a Family Group Conference on this day and agreed to complete the sanctions that Mrs. Barrett had written in a space below. The agreement form didn't say "or else" but it might as well have.

Once we had all signed the agreement, Mrs. Barrett said, "Before we conclude this circle, thank you all for your patience. I am a newly trained facilitator, and this has been my first circle. I was quite nervous."

"Me too."

She smiled at me. "I know you were, Darrah. But there's a big difference between us. I plan on attending many more circles; I'm sure this will be your only one. Now, I've brought juice and cookies. Please, everyone, help yourself."

I sat on my chair, not wanting to get up and join the adults who were chatting as they gathered around the food table, as if they were all suddenly best friends.

Mom brought Mrs. Johnson a cookie and a glass of juice then went back to talk to the others.

Mrs. Johnson sipped her juice and stared at something over my left shoulder. I looked, but no one was there. That seemed strange.

"Is this going to work?" she asked.

"What?"

She turned her head and peered directly at me through her thick glasses. "How about it? Are we going to get along? I know you don't want to do this, but I can use the help."

I shrugged. "Whatever."

She laughed. "You owe me, girl, and don't you forget it. Think you'd get off so easily if I told the real story of how I fell on those stairs? We both know you bumped into me."

My hands suddenly went cold, and my heart began racing. "Why didn't you tell them?" I whispered, afraid the constable would hear and change her mind about not sending me to court. But Constable Markes was busy munching on a cookie and talking to Mrs. Barrett. "Why didn't you tell them I made you fall?"

Mrs. Johnson finished her juice and put the glass carefully on the empty chair next to her. Then, still looking over my shoulder, she said softly, "You'll figure it out, kid. You're not dumb. You'll figure it out."

Chapter Five

AFTER A LONG, TENSE weekend, Mom picked me up from school on Monday and took me to begin my sanctions.

Mrs. Johnson lived on the edge of town, an older area where most of the homes had been built fifty years ago and were showing their age. Her place had a big wooden fence around it, so I couldn't see into the yard. All weekend I had been imagining fields of potatoes lurking in that yard, waiting for me to dig them up.

"Mind your manners, Darrah, and do whatever she asks without complaining. You understand that you have to do this, no matter how much you don't want to." One last reminder from Mom. Of course.

"Whatever."

"Don't say that. It's disrespectful."

"Whatever . . . whatever you say, Mom." I shut the car door as firmly as I could without actually slamming it.

Mom shouted out the open window. "Your father will be here at six, right after your two and a half hours are up. Be ready. I don't need both of you late for supper."

I didn't answer and she drove away. The gate in the fence had a metal latch that squeaked open. I swung the gate forward and back a few times, listening to the squeak, then took a deep breath, pushed it all the way open and stepped inside.

"You trying to make your mother angry?" Mrs. Johnson was in the yard, leaning against a rickety picnic table, her yellow toenails covered by a thick sock, her cane resting beside her. She had heard Mom and me outside the fence.

"I don't care if she's mad," I said. "Where are the potatoes?"

Mrs. Johnson looked puzzled. "Potatoes? Why?"

"I thought I was supposed to dig them up."

"You were, but I had Grandson Number Five do it on Saturday. Don't worry, I've got other things for you to do. Follow me." She levered herself off the table and hobbled towards the front door, cackling. "Oh, yes, things for you to do and your little dog, too."

Dog? I looked around. No dog. The woman was insane.

She waited for me at the top of a short flight of stairs which she'd slowly navigated while I was debating her sanity. I took a closer look at the house. It was painted a regular house colour, brown, but the half-dozen stairs leading up to the front door were pumpkin orange. Really, really bright orange, outlined in dark green on the edges of each step. A wrought-iron railing ran along both sides of the narrow stairs and it was also a dark green. Mrs. Johnson stood at the top of the orange stairs, waiting for me.

"Come on, girl. Hurry it up and don't look so bewildered. You've never seen *The Wizard of Oz*? Were you a deprived child? Click your heels together three times and come inside."

She was trying to be funny! Did my sanctions include having to laugh at her bad jokes?

"Let's go, Dorothy," I said to myself, sighing as I climbed the stairs which, though not a yellow brick road, still led me to a strange land. Would it be a house of horrors? Maybe she was a hoarder. Maybe she drank. Dorothy didn't have to worry about Tin Man being a hoarder or a drunk.

"Close the door behind you, no point in heating the whole outdoors." She disappeared inside.

I took a deep breath and stepped into—gingerbread. The smell of real gingerbread, the kind my grandmother used to make before Alzheimer's took her away.

"Come on, girl, get a move on. Take your shoes off, there's slippers in a basket by the door. Then come into the kitchen."

I hung my backpack and coat on a row of hooks on the wall, pulled on a pair of crocheted purple slippers (some other choices were pink with blue specks or the same shade of pumpkin orange as the stairs) and followed her voice into the kitchen.

No hoarding here. Everything was tidy, the floor gleamed, no dirty dishes in the sink, no piles of garbage. The kitchen was large, with lots of windows. The branches of a tree waved next to the big window behind the kitchen nook, and a plate of gingerbread, a bowl of whipped cream, a real cloth napkin and a single plate waited on the table.

"Thought you might be hungry," the woman said. "I'd join you, but with this cast, I can't wriggle my way onto those damned wooden benches. I'll take my tea standing up. Pour yourself a cup. It's herbal, blueberries and something else." She gestured toward a teapot beside her on the counter. Her mug was already half full.

I shook my head as I slid behind the table. "No tea. My dad will be here at six. Can we get started? Please?"

"Eat some gingerbread first. My daughter-in-law baked it, used my recipe, and sent it over with Grandkid Number Five when he came to do the potatoes. It's not bad, but she's not the world's best cook."

Way too much information. But the gingerbread smelled good, so I took a piece. All I wanted to do was get started on whatever evil chore she had planned for me. The gingerbread tasted the same as my grandmother's. Maybe it was the same recipe, one all grandmothers knew. My grandma would never have worn jeans like Mrs. Johnson, she always wore skirts or dresses and proper shoes, not like the old runner that Mrs. Johnson had on the foot of her unbroken leg. My grandma would never let her toenails get yellow and she would never plant potatoes. She had a rose garden in her backyard and she loved working in it. Even after she'd ripped out all the rose bushes on one of her bad days—guess her mixed-up mind thought they were weeds—she'd be out there, digging away in the bare dirt, big floppy hat to protect her from the sun, pink gardening gloves . . .

"Something wrong with your eyes? Or are you crying?"

"No." I wiped my face with the cloth napkin. It smelled of lavender. Like grandma's bedroom used to, before she had to go live in the hospital. I wished Mom would use cloth napkins but she said she had better things to do than try to get spaghetti stains out of napkins, and besides my brother's table manners didn't deserve cloth napkins. Maybe when he learned how to eat like a human being . . .

Without realizing it, I sighed again.

"You okay, girl?"

"I'm fine. What do you want me to do?"

"You're an actress, right?"

"Yes," I said, surprised by the question.

"So you read well. Aloud, I mean."

"Very well," I said. I wasn't feeling modest. "Why?"

"Put my glasses down somewhere, can't lay my hands on them. Wondered if you'd read me the paper."

"Don't you have something else you want me to do? Something you can't do with that sprained arm . . ." That was when I noticed the sling was gone.

"Wasn't much wrong with my arm," she said. "Just a few

aches and a big bruise. As long as I kept the sling on, my family pitched in. Like digging up the potatoes and making gingerbread."

"You lied at the circle!"

"Nope. I didn't say anything untrue. Everyone assumed. It did hurt for a while."

In spite of myself, I grinned. "I suppose you don't want me to tell Mrs. Barrett and the constable that your arm works just fine."

"I'd appreciate it if you didn't. Besides, you signed the agreement. You have to help me for fifty hours. Doesn't matter if I'm right as rain, you're still stuck with me."

My grin vanished. "Where's the newspaper you want me to read?"

"Right beside you. The top one of that pile. Just read the headlines and I'll tell you if I want you to read the whole thing."

I picked one up. It was the community paper, only a few pages long; underneath it was a stack of thicker newspapers, Saturday's *Globe and Mail* on the top.

Hoping I wouldn't have to read the whole lot of them, I scanned the headlines in the local paper and read aloud. "Injuries after Highway Collision."

"Nope, probably another drunk driver."

"Support from Green Party for Protest Against the New Mine."

"Lord, no. I've heard enough about that mine to last me a lifetime. Next."

I read headlines about rebates for "Power Smart Month," about how badly one of the political parties was doing in the polls, and a call for volunteers to organize a food bank drive.

"Nope, nope, nope."

"Homeless Tent City Near Railway Tracks."

"All right, that one sounds interesting."

It was a long article, and I took my time. Reading aloud beat scrubbing floors; I'd spin it out as much as I could.

"Our town has a new subdivision—at least that's what the homeless people who have erected a tent city of more than a dozen 'homes' told the media. 'We have nowhere else to go. We've got a couple of old barbecues so we can cook our own meals—the grocery stores throw out lots of good food. Sometimes people bring us vegetables from their gardens or rice, stuff like that.'

"When asked how long the new subdivision would be in-habited, a spokesperson replied, 'Until the city reopens the shelter they closed.' The chair of Citizens Against Poverty (C.A.P.) urged the city to restore funding for the homeless shelter in the old Queen Victoria Hotel. 'Winter is coming,' she said. 'We don't want another homeless person dying from exposure—please reopen that facility.' The mayor could not be reached for comment."

"That's a bunch of garbage," I said at the same time as Mrs. Johnston said, "That's nonsense."

"What?" Again, we both spoke at once.

"You go first," she said. "What makes you think a tent city is garbage?"

"Half of those people have homes to go to. They just don't want to be there. It's their choice to sleep on the streets. Some kids at my school go downtown on the weekend in grubby clothes with signs, like 'Help me, I'm starving.'"

"They're easy to spot. They have good teeth and clean fingernails. No one gives them money."

"That's not true! One girl made nearly a hundred dollars last weekend."

"That's only a few people. There are many others who are truly homeless."

"My dad says there's work for anyone who wants it. The people who beg are lazy."

"I disagree."

"There's 'help wanted' signs all over town, almost every store and restaurant is looking for help."

"Part-time at minimum wage, no doubt. Those jobs don't pay enough for a person to buy groceries, much less pay their rent."

I shrugged. "You said the article was nonsense. Why? I thought you agreed with me."

"I violently disagree. Our government spends money on parades, sports activities, hanging flower baskets, all kinds of things. But ask them to do some real good with the money rather than showing off, and they've got 'no comment.'"

"You're kidding. You think we should support the street people? My dad say half of them are drug addicts."

"Young lady, your father doesn't don't know what he's

talking about. Neither do you. Statistics show that many people who live on the streets do so because they are mentally ill. If we had more facilities to look after people like that, to make sure they take their medication, then . . ."

"That's not true. There are lots of places . . ."

"You're pretty opinionated for a young person, aren't you?"

"You're pretty opinionated for an . . ." I shut my mouth before I could say something I'd regret.

I guess Mrs. Johnson decided to keep any more opinions to herself, too. "Anything else interesting in that paper?" she asked.

There wasn't much more to read. "The classifieds? The obituaries? How am I supposed to know what you think is interesting?" I got up and poured myself some blueberry tea; my throat was scratchy. She held out her cup, and I topped it up for her.

My hands were black with ink from the paper. I went to the sink and washed them. "Why do you get so many newspapers? They're filthy." I watched the grey water from my hands circle around her clean sink.

"Not all newspapers smudge, not anymore. Some use a printing process that—"

"The one I was reading left my hands black."

"So keep washing until they're clean. It won't kill you."

"Why bother with newspapers and having to wash after you read them? We get news from the computer or TV. Sometimes on our phones."

She bristled. "Don't use the white towel, use the other one."

"Whatever." Even though I'd washed well, my hands left dark smudges on the blue towel.

"There are still people who prefer to get their news on real paper. I love my newspapers."

"They use up trees."

"So do books."

"Books last for years. A newspaper is going to be thrown out the next day. No point in wasting a natural resource on something so temporary."

"That something else your dad says?"

"Yes, but he's right. Besides, we've got e-readers, we don't need real books anymore."

"Ever consider that not everyone has a computer or an e-reader?"

"Oh, come on. Everyone does. Everyone who's normal."

"Well, then you're in an abnormal house with an abnormal woman. I have neither. Nor do I have a cellphone."

"You're kidding."

"Nope. Besides, newspapers can be recycled and used again. I use mine for mulch in the garden and for starting the fire in the fireplace."

"You're still using up trees. It's a waste."

"And toilet paper is made from what exactly? Is that a waste of trees, too?"

"We need toilet paper. We don't need newspapers, not anymore."

I glared at her and she glared back. There was a knock on the door, which was a good thing because I was angry and so was she.

"It's nearly six," said Mrs. Johnson. "That's probably your dad. Don't keep him waiting. You can see yourself out, and we can continue this conversation on Wednesday."

"Whatever," I said, heading for the front door.

I was so upset I walked outside in the purple slippers. Dad stared at my feet, astonished. I caught the door before it swung shut behind me and changed footgear. Once we were in the car, Dad asked, "Well, how did it go?"

"Stupid old woman," I said. "Thinks she knows everything."

Chapter Six

ON WEDNESDAY, MOM wasn't waiting to pick me up after school but there was a message on my cellphone. "I'm with Andrew at the hospital. He had a bad one, hit his head, the ambulance . . ." Her voice shook; she was crying. "Phone Mrs. Johnson and tell her you won't be there today, I'm at the hospital and can't pick you up to take you. Go home."

One of the doctors my parents took my brother to said that when Andrew reached puberty, his seizures could end. Another doctor told Mom that sometimes brain surgery could fix epilepsy, but they wouldn't consider surgery until they were sure they couldn't control the seizures with medication. So for now, medications were the only way to handle them, and they weren't working very well.

I thought about how all of our lives changed so much last spring when the school phoned to say that Andrew had been taken to the hospital, that he'd had a seizure. It was a warm day, like today, too warm for the early spring. Mom called me that day too, and told me to take the bus home, but my parents didn't come home for hours. No one let me know what was happening; I sat alone and waited. Andrew stayed in the hospital overnight, so did Mom. Then they sent him in an ambulance to Vancouver to see a specialist at the Children's Hospital. Mom went in the ambulance with him, but Dad and I drove down. I didn't want to go, but they didn't have time to "make arrangements" for me, so I had to go with Dad. I was nearly sixteen, I could have stayed in the house by myself.

We were gone a week. When we came home, I went back to school and so did Andrew. Everything was supposed to go back to normal, but it didn't because we had all transformed into the seizure police. Mom and Dad watched Andrew every second. If they went out, they left me with a list of instructions: who to call, what to do, what not to do, even what to say to him.

I crossed the street to the bus stop. The bus that was just pulling in was a number eight. On Wednesday, I'd seen that number bus stopping outside Mrs. Johnson's. Without thinking, I hopped on. Going to help a cranky, crazy old lady was better than going home to an empty house.

I wasn't more than a few minutes late. She was leaning against the picnic table again, face turned up, eyes closed.

"Got to get my sun while I can," she said, without opening her eyes. "In a few weeks, my garden will be in shade all day. Damn, I hate winters. Come, sit awhile. A dose of Vitamin D won't hurt you after being cooped up in school."

I propped myself up on the table beside her. With her head back, the wrinkles seemed to smooth out; she didn't look that old. Maybe it was the sunshine, washing her face with warmth. I put my own head back and shut my eyes, pretending it was still summer and I was at the beach.

We were both quiet for a while. Then I asked, "What do you want me to do today?" The front lawn was covered with leaves, and it was so nice outside I hoped she'd ask me to rake them. I didn't want to read more newspaper articles—not if she was going to be so opinionated about what we read.

"I've got a hankering for biscuits," she said. "You can make them."

"Biscuits?" I said, thinking of those dry cracker-like things my grandmother used to call "tea biscuits."

"You can buy them in the grocery store. Why do you want to make them?"

"Baking powder biscuits. With cheese. Hot from the oven. You can't buy those, young lady, except in a bakery, and they aren't as good as the ones I make."

"I don't do cooking. Except grilled cheese sandwiches."

"They don't make you take home economics in school anymore?"

"It's an elective. I take drama."

"Lord, what is our education system coming to?" She pushed herself away from the picnic table, standing for a moment to get her balance before heading inside. "How old are you again? Sixteen? A girl your age should be able to help out in the kitchen."

I shrugged. "We like takeout, especially when Mom's working."

"Takeout! Fat, salt and additives. What is your mother thinking?"

"She's busy, she's an accountant and she works part-time. She's been busier since Andrew . . ."

"Well, you're not busy, are you?"

"I don't want to cook. It's boring."

"Then I shall bore you thoroughly. Let's get started."

I chose the pumpkin orange slippers, in honour of the sunshine highlighting the yellow-orange leaves on the trees. These slippers were thicker than the purple ones, warmer. I shuffled into the kitchen, and Mrs. Johnson handed me a slim red book. It was so old that the insides were falling out; someone had taped the pages back in so long ago the tape was yellow and brittle. I read the title: *Foods, Nutrition and Home Management*, Revised 1955.

"What's this?"

"That little book contains everything a young woman needed to know about setting up and managing her home. It's a recipe book, a calorie counter, an etiquette guide and even has instructions for removing stains, washing silk garments and cleaning silver, linoleum, and windows. It also tells you how to make your own soup stock and lard."

"Yuck. You had to study stuff like that?"

I thumbed through the book, looking at some of the recipes: "Harvard Beets," "Escalloped Potatoes," "Lemon Snow," "Albumenized Water," "Finnan Haddie."

"Listen to this." I read aloud, "'Unit Four: Food Preparation, Personal Cleanliness. 1. A wash-dress or a dress well-covered with an apron is to be preferred. 2. The hair should be fastened with a band, so that no hairs may fall into the food while . . .' What's a wash-dress? What is this book?"

"This is my old Home Economics textbook. A wash dress is one that doesn't have to be dry-cleaned."

"They told you in school what to wear in your own kitchen? That's bizarre."

"I used those recipes a lot when I was first married. Didn't know how to cook anything except what I'd learned in Home Ec. It came in handy."

"'Escalloped Vegetables,' 'Franconia Potatoes' . . . are these Julia Child's recipes?"

"You saw the movie, right? No, it's nothing like her cookbooks. This is a text, an instructional manual. Back in those days, not many women went out into the world to work. Their work was considered running a household, and supplying a family with healthy, nutritious and inexpensive meals. Julia's recipes used a lot of butter, which was expensive when this book was first published, probably ten years before that 'new' edition."

I was flipping through the book again. "'Rules for Serving without a Maid.' Maid?"

"Some girls married rich men and had household help. Same as today."

"'Lighting the Coal Stove.' You're kidding. People used coal in their stoves? It pollutes."

"We used electric stoves in the Home Economics room at school, but many houses still had wood—or coal-fired—cook stoves. I never had to use one, thank heavens."

"'Care of Refrigerator and Cooler: keep the ice compartment filled at least one half.' They must have served tons of iced drinks in those days."

She laughed. "The ice was to keep the food cold. Although there were electric refrigerators when this book was first published, some families still used ice boxes. Those were insulated 'boxes' with a big chunk of ice in them to keep everything cold."

"Like a picnic cooler?"

"Exactly. But the ice boxes had a drip pan you had to empty every day, and ice was delivered to your house. I remember the ice man coming to our house. He had huge tongs with pointed ends to grab the block of ice. Then he'd sling it over his shoulder and carry it in."

"You're really old, aren't you?"

"You're really rude, aren't you?"

I felt my cheeks going red. "I'm sorry. I didn't mean 'old,' I meant . . ."

"Nice try, but I think 'old' is exactly what you meant. You

can be extremely tactless, you know."

"I'm sorry, Mrs. J."

"Mrs. J? Why did you call me that?"

"Sorry, it just sort of slipped out, Mrs. Johnson."

"It's all right. I think I like it. Now, turn to page ninety and let's get started."

I found the recipe for baking powder biscuits and read it out loud. "Two cups of bread flour, one-half teaspoon salt, four teaspoons baking powder ..."

"Four teaspoons? No wonder mine didn't rise the last time, I thought it was ... Go on."

"Two to four tablespoons fat, two-thirds of a cup of milk. Follow the general rules." I looked at her blankly. "What rules?"

"Turn back a page."

There were eight general rules. Number one was "see to oven" (I guess that meant firing up the stove with coal or wood), and the final one was "bake 15-20 minutes." In between were instructions for adding stuff, mixing and kneading. *Okay*, I thought, *that doesn't sound too hard.*

Mrs. Johnson hoisted herself up to perch on the tall stool and pointed. "In that bottom cupboard there's a stack of white bowls. Bring them to me and I'll show you which one to use." Kneeling down, I found the stack of bowls. Once I had put them on the table, she tilted her head to one side, looked at them carefully then pointed to one in the middle.

"This should do."

She directed me to the cupboard where I found flour, to the fridge for lard (good thing I wasn't vegetarian) and to the drawer where the measuring cups and spoons were kept. She knew where everything was, right down to the exact shelf in the refrigerator where the cheese was stored.

I sifted flour, added "the leavening agent" (baking powder) and used two knives to cut the lard (the "fat" the recipe instructions called it) into the flour until it was the consistency of oatmeal. I'd never felt uncooked oatmeal, so I kept passing the bowl back to Mrs. J. until she declared it perfect.

Kneading the dough was easy, but rolling it out was a challenge. "Too thick; not thick enough; don't work it too hard or it will get tough." She rejected half a dozen sample pieces before declaring that I finally had the right thickness. Reaching into a cupboard above the counter where she sat, she pulled out a heavy drinking glass. "Don't know where my biscuit cutter is at the moment. Use this glass to cut the biscuits. It's a bit small, but the shape's perfect."

By the time the kitchen filled with the smell of baking biscuits, I had flour on my nose and dough in my hair. I'd wiped my hands along my jeans without realizing it, and noticed that they, too, were dusted with flour. Mrs. J. laughed at me.

"You better go clean up," she said. "Before your father gets here."

"He's probably not coming," I said, belatedly realizing that I hadn't left my parents a message telling them where I'd gone. With any luck they weren't home yet. Mom and Dad had stupid rules about knowing where I was every second of every day. Once, when I walked to school, Mom phoned me twice before I got there—during a twenty-minute walk!

I guess my panic showed. "Trouble?" she asked.

"My parents. They don't know I'm here. I have to call them right now." Floury hands and all, I dashed for my phone in the front hall, getting white hand prints all over my backpack.

Mom answered. "Darrah, where are you? I've been frantic. You're not answering your phone and I've checked with all your friends."

"I thought I should do my sanctions anyway," I tried to explain. "So I took the bus. My phone was in my backpack in the front hall; I didn't hear it."

"Well, you're not taking a bus home; it's almost dark. I'll send your father over to get you. He can pick up a pizza on the way back."

She didn't sound too mad, in spite of her words. "Sorry, Mom. I got busy and forgot to call."

My mother had already hung up. I'd have to apologize again when I got home.

I detoured by the bathroom and cleaned up a bit. Mrs. J. was trying to bend down far enough to peer into the oven. "You look," she said. "Tell me if you think they're golden brown on top."

They were. They were also double their original size. I grabbed the oven mitts and pulled out the pan. I'd used the biscuit recipe variation in the red book and made cheese biscuits, and the golden tops of the biscuits were speckled with flecks of grated cheddar.

"These smell good."

She told me where to find the cooling racks, and sniffed appreciatively as I took the biscuits off the pan. "Pass me one, please."

I did, and watched nervously as she broke it in half, blew on it, then took a bite. "Ah," she sighed. "That hits the spot. Almost as good as if I'd made them myself."

I beamed, as proud as if I'd landed the lead in a play. I had just taken my first bite when Dad banged at the door. I inhaled the rest of the biscuit. "See you on Monday," I said.

"Don't rush off, have another one. After all, you made them."

"I should go." I knew I was in for one of Dad's lectures on the "always letting your parents know where you are" theme. No point in making him wait to deliver it; he'd get madder.

"Invite him in," said Mrs. Johnson.

"Maybe it's not a good idea."

"Maybe it's an excellent idea. Bet he hasn't had a fresh biscuit since he left home and married your mom."

It turned out that Dad hadn't had homemade biscuits in years. He wolfed down two, and didn't object when Mrs. Johnson insisted I wrap up a half dozen more to take home.

"How's Andrew?" I asked as soon as we got in the car.

"He's got stitches where he hit his head, but he's okay, I think. He doesn't want to talk, shut himself up in his room when we got home from the hospital. Your mother thinks he's crying but he won't let her come in. She's upset and doesn't know what to do."

Then he remembered to be mad. "She's got enough on her mind without having to worry about where you are, Darrah. You know the rules."

But he said it mildly, and nodded absently when I apologized.

"Think you could make those biscuits at home?" he asked.

Chapter Seven

ANDREW NEVER CRIES. I mean, not since he was little. The last time I remember him crying was his first day of kindergarten. Mom drove us both to school and went in with him, but she had to go to work. She couldn't stay like most of the other mothers, so she took Andrew to his classroom, hung out for a half hour, then left.

Shortly after she left, Andrew arrived at my classroom door, bawling his eyes out. The principal was with him. "Darrah, can we borrow you for a few minutes?" I ended up spending the rest of the morning in the kindergarten room, holding Andrew's hand until snack time when he let go long enough to grab and eat a happy-face cupcake. At the end of the kindergarten day, which was lunch time for the rest of the school, I took him outside where he clung to me until Mom arrived and lifted him into the car.

The next morning, he took a deep breath, opened the car door, got out and marched across the playground without looking back.

"Andrew? Do you want Darrah to come with you?" Mom shouted at his back. He turned around briefly and called, "No, I can do this." Next thing I knew, he was on top of the monkey bars, hanging upside down. Two little girls were staring up at him with silly looks on their faces. He wasn't crying.

Now he's in grade five, plays soccer, wins ribbons at sports days and is always covered with bruises and cuts because he throws himself completely into whatever game he is playing. But I'm almost positive he hasn't cried since his first day of school.

Tonight he was crying. I stood outside his bedroom door and listened. The sound was faint, muffled, as if he were sobbing into a pillow, but he was definitely crying.

"Talk to him, Darrah," pleaded Mom. "Find out what's wrong. Every time I ask him he says, 'Nothing.' I told him we had pizza for dinner and he said he wasn't hungry. See if you can find out what's going on."

I didn't think Andrew would talk to me about why he was crying; we're not exactly close. He leads his life and I lead mine; the five and a half years between us separate our lives so much that they don't intersect very often. Our parents make me go to his soccer games if he's in a tournament and insist that he comes to see any play I'm in, but we don't "talk."

I looked behind me. Mom stood at the foot of the stairs, making "go on" gestures with her hands. I knocked on his door. "Andrew?"

No answer.

"Can I come in?"

No answer, but the sobs grew quieter.

"Please, tell us what's wrong."

"Go away, Dar."

"Andrew? Remember your first day of kindergarten? How scared you were? Remember I came with you and the next day you weren't scared anymore?"

"You just wanted a happy face cupcake," he said.

"That's right, I got a cupcake at snack time, too. Mine was blue and pink. Yours was green with a big white smile."

Silence. Then a grudging, "Okay, come in."

Andrew was huddled on his bed, clutching a damp pillow. He wiped his nose on his sleeve, then tried to grin. There was a bandage on his forehead and he looked almost as white as it was. "No cupcakes here, Dar. Just the zombie."

"What do you mean?" I sat down on the bed beside him.

"Today, while the ambulance guys were wheeling me out of the school, I woke up. The blood was running down in my eyes and they were holding something on my head to catch the blood and Mom was there and she was saying . . ."

"'Oh, Andrew, oh, Andrew, oh, Andrew?'"

"How did you guess?" He almost grinned.

"And?"

"All the kids were in the hallways and on the steps outside because it was lunch hour, and they watched the ambulance people take me away. I kept saying I could walk, please let me walk, but the first-aid people kept pushing me on that wheeled stretcher and wouldn't let me. This one grade seven guy, he's hanging over the stairs and he says, 'It's zombie time again.' Then he goes cross-eyed and sticks out his tongue and everyone laughed."

"Oh."

"They call me 'Seizure Salad.' I hate that name."

"Oh." I wasn't doing well in the talking department; I didn't know what to say.

"Darrah?"

"When I have a seizure, what happens?"

"Uh ..." I wasn't too sure myself. "There's some broken connection in your brain and ..."

"I don't want medical stuff. I mean, what do I do? When I wake up I can't remember anything, there's this blank, like time got swallowed up in a black hole. What do I do when it happens?"

"It's not much to look at."

"Liar. There's a video clip on one of the medical sites. I saw someone jerking all over and drooling when they were having a seizure—is that what I do?"

I swallowed hard. "Sort of. But it's not gross."

He looked hard at me. "Honestly?"

"Uh . . . you thrash around a bit."

"I always fall down," he said. "This time I hurt my arm as well as my head, but I didn't tell anyone about the arm. They were all worried about my bleeding head." He touched it gently. "Four stitches!"

"Way to go, I guess. Let's see your arm."

"What's to see except a bruise? You're not a doctor, you're trying to change the subject. Tell me the truth. What do I look like? Do I do funny things with my eyes?"

"Sometimes," I admitted. "But sometimes you just close them."

"Do I look stupid?"

"No. Honestly, Andy, it's more frightening than gross. We all feel helpless; there's not a lot we can do except wait. The doctors told us to stay calm. Actually, mostly we try to keep Mom calm. You know how she is."

Andrew smiled.

"And we make sure you don't hurt yourself."

He looked puzzled. "How?"

"We put something soft under your head and move furniture so you don't thrash into it. Then you go limp and fall asleep. Sometimes you sleep for a long time. Mom cries and keeps saying—"

"'Oh, Andrew, oh, Andrew, oh, Andrew?'"

My turn to grin. "How did you ever guess?"

He hugged the pillow against him. "I'm not allowed to do anything anymore. I miss soccer."

"That's just until they find the right medication. Then you can do everything you used to."

"That's what the doctor says. But I have to try out a new drug for weeks and then have more tests to see if it's working. Soccer will be over before I can play. I'm going to miss everything!"

"It will work out, give it time."

"I don't want to give any more time to this stupid disease! It's not fair. The first medicine the doctor put me on made me so tired I fell asleep at school."

"I remember that. You fell asleep at the dinner table too, right into your mac and cheese."

"This new drug, I feel like I'm shivering inside all the time. My hands shake. I hit the wrong keys on the keyboard, lost half an assignment last week because I hit delete and didn't realize it."

"Everyone does that."

"Not all the time."

Mom poked her head into the room. "How's it going?" she asked cheerfully.

"You didn't knock!" I said. "Were you listening?"

"Oh, of course not, I would never—"

Andrew glared at her. "You're supposed to knock. That's a family rule."

"Sorry. I wondered if . . ." She stopped, looked from one of us to the other. "If . . ." She stopped again.

We waited. "If what?" I finally asked.

"If you're ready to, uh, eat dinner?"

"We'll be down in a minute."

She backed out of the room, shutting the door behind her. I pulled the pillow away from Andrew; reluctantly he let go. "Come on."

"I don't want pizza again! We had it twice last week. I'm not hungry."

"You know she'll keep at you until you eat something."

"Don't want to."

"Want to try a cheese biscuit with butter and jam?"

"Cheese biscuit?"

"Wash your face and come downstairs and I'll give you one," I said, hoping fervently that Dad hadn't eaten all of them. "You'll like it, I promise."

Mom and Dad were waiting for us, the pizza box was on the table, dinner was served. The box looked greasy; I suddenly wasn't hungry either. Maybe I'd open a can of chicken noodle soup instead.

"It's so good to hear the two of you talking," said Mom, smiling and hugging us.

"Mom!" Andrew pushed her away. "Don't helicopter."

"Sit down, let's eat," said Dad.

"Go ahead," I headed for the kitchen.

There were two biscuits left. I found the butter and jam and gave the biscuits a few seconds in the microwave to warm. Then I brought them into the dining room and announced, "I baked them myself. Try one."

"Poison, poison, spare me, evil sister." Andrew threw his hands up over his face and pretended to cower. I thrust the plate under his nose. He sniffed, grabbed a biscuit and took a bite.

"Hey, not bad for poison. Did you really make them?"

There were still traces of tears on his cheeks. For a moment I thought I was back in that kindergarten room with a five-year-old brother clutching my hand. It was a good memory.

◆ ◆ ◆

Andrew was himself again by the weekend. He'd pulled the bandage off so the stitches showed—ugly black threads with the ends sticking out like spider legs over the angry slash of the cut. When Mom made a fuss, wanting to put another bandage on him, he ignored her. "It really is gross," I said.

"Good. Don't look." Things were back to normal, whatever normal was in our house these days.

Andrew asked for more cheese biscuits. I didn't have Mrs. Johnson's recipe, but I found a recipe on the internet that sounded the same and made biscuits for Sunday dinner. Mom cooked a roast and bought some macaroni salad. She insists we eat dinner together, the whole family—she read somewhere that doing that will keep your teenagers off drugs, or something equally bizarre. So unless someone has a meeting or a game or a rehearsal, we always sit at the dining-room table and eat dinner together. But usually dinner wasn't this fancy, with a roast and my biscuits.

Dad and Andrew ate so many biscuits I moved the remainder beside my plate. "You're both cut off until Mom and I have had our share."

"Maybe there will be some left for breakfast," said Andrew.

Dad nodded. "If only we had some strawberry jam like my mother used to make ..." He saw the look on Mom's face and shut up.

"I'll see what I can find at the farmer's market," she said, her voice tight.

"Maybe Darrah can learn how to make jam," said Dad. "Do you suppose your Mrs. Johnson can teach you how?"

"I can make it by myself. There's recipes on the net, I'll look one up."

"Why don't you stick to making biscuits and try to enjoy the jam I buy from you know, one of those stores where they sell food? Not every woman is born wanting to make jam," said Mom.

Dad and I looked guiltily at each other. Mom could be sensitive about her cooking—or rather her lack of cooking. "I have a job outside the home," she said. "I do my best, but I don't have time to make jam. Or biscuits."

◆ ◆ ◆

Monday afternoon I was back at Mrs. J.'s.

"Jam?" she said, horrified. "You're not ready, not nearly. Besides, I gave away my jars and canner last year. It got too hard to clean the fruit. Got two big flies in my last batch of peach jam; decided it was time to give it up."

"Are we going to cook?" Again the house was spotless, clean blue and white tea towels hanging by the sink, the crocheted slippers nesting tidily in their basket, the kitchen floor swept. There were no area mats in the kitchen or anywhere else that I had seen. No place to hide dust.

"Not today. You can read me the paper."

"Still can't find your glasses? Want me to look for them?"

"No, leave it be. Just read."

The town's twice-weekly paper was the only newspaper on the kitchen bench; Mrs. J. must have been recycling. Or else she'd had her grandson put the other papers in the garden, for, what was it she said, "mulch"? Curious, I asked.

"I cancelled my subscriptions," she said. "Can't get around to reading everything these days."

"I could read them to you."

"No thanks. You're only going to be with me a few weeks. What will I do after you've gone? Besides, it isn't the same as reading by yourself."

"Sorry." I was miffed and my voice showed it.

"You're a good reader, it isn't that. But I miss . . ." She stopped and sighed. "So put on your best stage voice and try to make local politics sound interesting."

There wasn't much in the paper this week. The tent city was being dismantled by the RCMP, the mayor was looking for funding to reopen the old hotel that used to be a homeless shelter; the columnist was going on about problems in the schools. There was, for a change, nothing about the controversial gold and copper mine that was to be built a few miles out of town. Even the most outspoken writer of letters to the editor had taken the week off.

I finished reading long before six. "What should I do now?"

"Go scrub your hands, in the bathroom this time, not in the kitchen sink. Then let's go for a walk."

"Walk?"

"Just around the back of the house. I want to check on the garden."

The bathroom was as clean as the rest of the house, the old-fashioned sink sparkling, the linoleum on the floor spotless, no floss specs on the mirror. I stole a look at the plastic seat perched high over the regular toilet seat—her throne. There was a night light by the sink, in the shape of a bouquet of glass flowers, and it made the counter sparkle with white and yellow light. In the front hallway was a similar night light, red and white, and a soft purple and white one in the hallway.

When I finished, Mrs. J. was already outside the door, a brightly coloured shawl over her shoulders, a knit cap in the same pattern pulled down around her ears, her cane in hand. I pulled on my coat and shoes. She made me make sure I'd tied my shoes properly so I wouldn't trip and pull her down with me when I fell. We moved slowly along a narrow, cracked cement path. I felt her grab me a few times to keep her balance, but we navigated the path safely and turned the corner.

She stopped by a weathered wooden bench under a big tree. The leaves were gone. Even though it had been a mild fall, most of the trees had given up their leaves by the middle of October. Mrs. J. slowly lowered herself down to the bench. "I miss my garden. Sit here a lot in the summer, it's shady and quiet. Good spot to think."

"It's too cold to think today. Can we go in?"

"In a minute." She looked over at the square of earth. "I usually turn it over myself but couldn't handle the pitchfork this year. Love the smell of the earth."

I sniffed, but couldn't smell anything special. The small garden had been dug up, "turned over," and the earth looked damp. A few spiky things, sort of like green onion tops but bent over, clumped together in one corner.

"Perennial onions." Mrs. J. was pointing to the spiky clump. "Make new little onion bulbs right on top of each stem. I used to pick them off and use them in my mustard pickles. Haven't made pickles in years."

"Maybe you can teach me?"

"Perhaps. But it's too late in the season to get good pickling cukes. Besides, I think my pickling days are over."

Then she looked away from the garden and changed the subject. "Did I tell you Mrs. Barrett called me?"

"Why?"

"Just to see how things are going."

"She's checking up on me?"

"Perhaps."

"I'm doing my sanctions. I signed the agreement, didn't I?"

"She also wanted to find out how we are getting along."

"Oh. What did you tell her?"

"It doesn't matter. She was content."

"She didn't have to call you."

"It's not worth getting mad about. I think it's just a follow-up, probably a rule of this circle thing."

"She's treating me like I'm a criminal." Oops. What had the little constable said about me breaking a part of the Criminal Code of Canada? I was a criminal.

We were both silent for a while. Then she asked, "Want to tell me why you were so upset that day at the hospital? It was more than missing the audition, wasn't it?"

"No." I stared at the clumps of dirt that would be a garden in the summer. There was a scattering of frost clinging to the bigger lumps, like an uneven dusting of white. Suddenly I felt colder.

"Are you sure you don't want to talk about it?"

"It was nothing."

"Really? Seems strange that 'nothing' made you so angry."

I was relieved when Dad poked his head around the corner of the house. "I thought I heard voices," he said. "Evening, Mrs. Johnson. No biscuits today?"

"I hear you ate a lot of them. They must have been acceptable."

"They were."

"She's just beginning. Wait a few weeks and see what the girl can cook."

Dad helped Mrs. J. back down the path and up the stairs; she leaned on his arm as if she were tired, although we hadn't been out for long.

"Thank you," she said from the front porch. "Goodnight to you both."

"You're welcome, Mrs. J.," I said. "Take care of yourself."

"You too."

"Sounds as if things are going well," Dad said as we drove off.

"She's okay. For an old lady."

"For an old lady with a broken leg which was your fault, I'd say she's more than just 'okay.'"

I stared out the window and was quiet the rest of the way home.

Chapter Eight

WEDNESDAY, I PEELED potatoes and carrots, cleaned and chopped celery and onions, browned chunks of meat and put a stew on to simmer. The next week I did more cooking: shepherd's pie on Monday (mushy hamburger with mashed potatoes on top), and Wednesday I made chicken soup, starting with raw chicken legs. I didn't like taking the meat off the chicken bones very much; it was greasy and looked gross. But the soup I left cooking for Mrs. J.'s dinner smelled good, not at all like canned stuff.

On Saturday, a strange thing happened. I got a phone call from a boy. That didn't used to be strange. I had a boyfriend last year, but so far this school year I hadn't even thought about one. Can't go out on dates when you're grounded. Can't keep a relationship going when you have to use the phone in the kitchen with everyone listening.

Mom looked puzzled as she handed me the phone. "He says his name is Robin."

"I don't know any Robins. What does he want?"

"I didn't ask him that," she snapped. "Last time I asked someone's name, you called me an interrogator from the Spanish Inquisition."

"Why didn't he call my cell?"

"Ask him yourself."

"Hello? This is Darrah."

"Oh, hi, I'm Mrs. Johnson's grandson."

"Grandkid Number Five?"

He was silent for a moment. "How did you know that?"

"What do you want, Number Five? Are you Five of Nine? You related to Seven?"

"No, there are only five of us. It's Five of Five. You like *Voyager*, too?"

"I like *Next Generation* better, but I've been watching both lately. So, what do you want in my universe, Five of Five?"

"I'm calling for my grandma. She invited friends for tea on Sunday, and she wondered if you'd come after lunch and help her. Make gingerbread, set the table and stuff like that, I guess."

I didn't say anything. He spoke into the silence. "You are the girl who's been helping her, right? Grandma said something about a school work experience program."

"Something like that." He didn't know why I was really doing those hours. Thank you for that, Mrs. J.

"Glad I got the right person."

"You did. And you're the person who dug up her potatoes so I didn't have to. I owe you."

He laughed. "There weren't many. Grandma's garden has been getting smaller and smaller every year. It didn't even take an hour to get those spuds up and washed."

"I'll have to ask my mom about Sunday."

"I can pick you up and bring you back. I'm invited for tea, too, but probably only because she wants me to run taxi service for her friends."

Mom had been hovering, listening hard. It had been months since a boy had called me, and she was having a hard time keeping her curiosity in line. "Can I go to Mrs. Johnson's tomorrow, Mom?"

"Will that count as time towards your sanction hours?"

"I don't know. Her grandson will pick me up and bring me back."

She raised her eyebrows, mouthing "grandson?" I nodded and went back to the phone.

"Okay, Robin, I'm cleared."

"I'll pick you up at one, if that's okay."

"No need to come in; I'll be watching for you." I rattled off our address, then hung up.

"Make sure you keep a record of these extra hours," Mom said. "You might need to take an afternoon off sometime or—"

"Mom, drop it."

"I wonder why she didn't call you herself?" Mom stared at me thoughtfully and I stormed off. Why did it matter who phoned? It wasn't as if this was a date or anything.

◆ ◆ ◆

Robin drove an old Honda CRV, silver. It had scrapes and bumps on one side and a big dent in the front, but the inside was clean and comfortable.

"Nice ride." I was being sarcastic, but he took me seriously.

"It works for me. Actually, it's grandma's car. Wouldn't be my choice, but the price was right—free—and she pays the insurance and buys some of the gas. All I have to do is take her grocery shopping once in a while or drive her to visit one of her friends."

"Doesn't she drive it?"

"She can't with that cast. She wouldn't drive at night even before her fall. After that accident, she gave me the car and put me on speed dial. Now I drive her everywhere."

Not wanting to talk about the "accident," I changed the subject. "I don't even have my learner's. You're lucky."

"Aren't you old enough?"

"Yes, but . . ." I wasn't going to tell him that part of my punishment for the hospital disaster was that I couldn't even think about getting a driver's license for a year. "So, Five of Five, what else do you watch besides *Star Trek* reruns?" (Changing the subject again.)

We talked about sitcoms for the rest of the trip. Safe subject. When we got there, Robin came into the house with me, but Mrs. J. sent him right out again, to rake the leaves on the front lawn.

"Make sure you put the rake back in the shed when you're done. Then I'll tell you where to pick up my guests."

He saluted. "Yes ma'am. Right away, ma'am," and scurried back out.

At the kitchen door I stopped and stared. The usually tidy room was a mess; the floor covered with cookbooks, cooking magazines, recipes on loose-leaf paper, recipes on small cards, recipes torn from magazines or newspapers, a paper snowfall blanketing the kitchen.

Mrs. J. made her way carefully through the mess to the tall stool by the counter and perched on it. "What are you waiting for? Start picking them up. You know I can't bend down with this damned cast."

"Sorry," I mumbled, and began gathering the books. She didn't say a word until I had everything off the floor and stacked on the counter.

"Do you want me to put them away?"

She gestured. "Second cupboard from the sink. Middle shelf."

I started transferring books. "How did they fall out?"

"Didn't fall. I threw them."

"Really?"

"Of course, 'really.' Are you stupid today? Couldn't find

what I was looking for, got mad and flung the whole lot on the floor."

I giggled. "I wish I'd seen that!"

She managed a small smile. "It wasn't pretty, be glad you missed it."

"What were you looking for?"

"My Home Ec. book, the red one."

"*Foods, Nutrition and Home Management*?"

"Yes."

"It's right here, on the bench, beside the newspaper."

"What fool left it there?"

"Me. I'm sorry."

"Never mind, I'm glad it's found. Okay, page 89, gingerbread, let's get started."

I read the ingredients aloud. "Molasses? What's that?"

"Thick, brown and sweet. Can't believe you've never seen molasses."

"Mom doesn't bake."

"Of course she doesn't. Read the gingerbread instructions."

"It just says, 'Mix according to the Muffin Method.' Muffin Method?"

"Basically, you try not to stir things too much . . ."

I had found the rules in the book. "'Make a depression in the flour, pour in egg, milk, then melted fat.' When do you put in the ginger?"

"With the flour and baking powder, of course. You always sift the dry ingredients together. This is dried powdered ginger, not the fresh root that they use in Chinese food.

"I know what root ginger is. We eat a lot of Chinese."

"Right, the takeout. I should have known. Now, get out the biggest mixing bowl, and one of the square cake pans from the same cupboard."

Mrs. J. didn't have me follow the ingredients exactly. We put in more powdered ginger and less brown sugar, and we used plain flour instead of the pastry flour the recipe called for. I didn't know there were different flours for breads and cakes. The molasses was so thick I couldn't get it to pour into a measuring cup, so I stuck the jar, without its lid, in the microwave for a few seconds, then it poured out easily.

"I'll have to remember that. Good idea, faster than standing the jar in warm water."

Robin came into the kitchen, had a glass of milk, sniffed the baking gingerbread and sighed. "How long until it's ready?"

"Soon. Show the girl where my sterling silver is and get out the teapot and five cups, the good ones from the china cabinet. The two of you can set the table in the dining room, use my lace tablecloth and the napkins that match. Then go pick up my guests while we get the kettle going and whip the cream."

I'd whipped cream before, for hot chocolate, so I had no problem doing that chore. When I pulled out the beaters, I handed one to Mrs. J. and licked the other one myself.

"Perfect," she announced. "Not too much sugar."

I beamed. "Thanks."

The gingerbread was cut into squares, the cream spooned into a bowl and the silver teapot filled with hot water, warming. "The only way to draw out all the flavour is with a pre-warmed pot," Mrs. J. said. She didn't use tea bags, just cans of loose tea. The one she had me bring down from the cupboard had a Chinese design on it. I opened the lid and sniffed. "It smells like flowers."

"It's Jasmine. Usually I prefer Oolong, but I thought you might enjoy this. The cosy is in the drawer with the tea towels, next to the sink."

I found the "cosy"—a crocheted cover for the teapot which would keep the tea warm. It was brightly striped in a pattern like Mrs. J.'s shawl and cap and topped with a big multi-coloured pom-pom. On each side was a hole (one for the spout, one for the handle), otherwise she could have worn it as a hat on cold days.

"My grandma had one of these, but it wasn't crocheted."

"I made this one. Can't find cozies in many stores. When you do they're artsy fancy and cost a fortune. These days almost everyone uses tea bags and makes their tea right in the cup. Revolting!"

The doorbell rang, and I was instructed to see the guests in. They were obviously frequent visitors, for they slipped off their shoes and chose slippers from the basket. Once they were ready, I ushered in a short, red-haired woman and a tall older man who walked with a brass-headed cane.

Mrs. J. was already seated at the head of the table. "These are my friends: Karen MacDonald, who helps me keep this old house clean, and David Allen, who is my square-dance partner."

"Used to be, until a few months ago when both of us had to give up dancing. I'm pleased to meet you, Darrah. Janie tells us you are becoming a competent cook. She shared some of the stew you made last week. It was excellent."

"Thank you." They used to dance together and they shared meals? Was this Mr. Allen her boyfriend? Did old people have boyfriends or girlfriends? I'd never thought about that before.

"I'm glad you're here to help Janie, Darrah," said Mrs. MacDonald. It sounds like a good program your school has."

Mrs. Johnson grinned. "It's a tremendous program. Now, bring in the tea, girl."

In the kitchen, I poured out the teapot's warming water, spooned in five teaspoons of the loose tea (one teaspoon per person, according to Mrs. J.'s instructions) poured the hot water into the pot, popped on the cosy and carried it to the dining room table. I set it on the hot pad in front of Mrs. Johnson, but she shook her head. "Let Karen pour, please. Then sit down."

I moved the hot pad and teapot to Mrs. MacDonald's place and sat down, worried about what I would say to these people. But I didn't need to say anything; everyone else talked. And talked.

Robin talked about his plans for university next year; Karen about her yoga classes, complaining of a sore back; Mr. Allen about the latest mystery series on PBS; and Mrs. J. asked everyone questions. I couldn't have squeezed a word in, even if I'd wanted to say something.

The tea tasted like flowers, like summer sunshine. The gingerbread was still warm and even better than the last time, probably because I was eating it from a thin china plate with roses in shades of pink and red around its edge. The teacup had matching roses on its rim; it was also thin, almost translucent so you could just about see the tea through the sides of the cup. The cream jug and sugar bowl had the same rose pattern as the dishes.

I ran my fingers over the rim of the gingerbread plate; the flowers were slightly raised.

Mrs. J. saw me. "Pretty, isn't it? This tea set was hand-painted by my grandmother for her hope chest."

"Painted?" I asked

"Hope chest?" asked Robin at the same time.

The adults smiled. Mrs. J. explained, "Those were actual 'chests,' often made of cedar, and a hopeful young woman, as in 'hoping to be married,' filled the chests with things she had made or collected, things she hoped to use proudly in her own house one day."

Mr. Allen took over. "The china was bought already glazed, but perfectly plain. Women spent hours designing and painting patterns with a special kind of paint. I believe the dishes were then put in a kiln or the oven and—"

"Your grandmother painted the flowers on this, Mrs. J?"

"On every single one of the eight cups, saucers, side plates —on everything."

"Wow!" said Robin, lifting his empty plate up to look more closely.

"Careful with that. It's French china—Limoges. Besides being valuable it will eventually be inherited by one of you five grandkids."

"Uh . . . no thanks, Gran. I'll pass on the china."

"Don't be hasty. Your wife may think differently."

"Wife?" The horrified look on his face made everyone laugh.

"Aha, so there's no romantic interest in your life right now, young man. But wait a few years." Mr. Allen smiled that superior smile adults use when they think they know more than you do, as if they are saying, "You'll understand when you're older." Mom uses that smile a lot.

"No problem, I can wait," Robin said. "Just watch me."

He carefully passed his cup to Mrs. Smith. "Any more tea?" he asked.

"Lots, but it's getting leafy near the bottom of the pot. Janie, where's your tea strainer?" She started to get up, but Mrs. J. motioned for me to go instead.

"Top left-hand drawer beside the sink," she said. "It's silver and sits in a little silver dish."

"I know what a tea strainer looks like." There was no need to talk down to Robin and me just because we're young. Describing a tea strainer, honestly.

I yanked open the drawer. No tea strainer. But at least four pairs of glasses, and a dozen magnifying glasses. Some small, some large, some with handles like the one Sherlock Holmes used. One square one was made of plastic, and was large enough to cover a whole page of a book. Another square one was attached to a strap, as if you hung it around your neck and peered through it.

Forgetting about the strainer, I grabbed a couple of pairs of glasses and called, "Mrs. J., I found—"

"Don't shout girl, it's rude. Come in here and say what you have to say."

I had taken two steps toward the dining room when something made me stop. The glasses were all together, in the same drawer. Mrs. Johnson knew where everything was; how could she not know her glasses were here?

I turned around, went back and slowly pulled open the next drawer. There was the silver tea strainer, right beside the coffee filters. I took it out, shut that drawer, and again pulled out the drawer beside it, the one I'd opened by mistake.

For a moment I stared at the collection of glasses and magnifiers, then I put the two pairs of glasses I'd picked out back and shut the drawer. I didn't know why Mrs. Johnson wanted to pretend she had lost her glasses, but for now, I'd play her game.

"Coming, Mrs. J.," I called, and went back to the tea party.

Chapter Nine

MRS. JOHNSON SENT me home early and didn't offer to give me any of the gingerbread. I had hoped she would.

"Don't dawdle," she said to Robin.

"Don't worry, Gran. I'll be back soon to take your friends home."

"Do you need help cleaning up, Mrs. Johnson? I don't mind staying longer." Maybe I'd end up with the left-over gingerbread if I helped in the kitchen.

"Not today, girl. Karen and I will do it. Get on home with you."

As we headed for the front hall and our jackets, we heard Mr. Allen objecting. "You'll not do dishes, Janie. I will; I know how to clean up a kitchen."

"Thank you for the offer, David, but I'd prefer that Karen did the washing and drying."

"Sit, the both of you. I can handle it alone." I could hear Mrs. MacDonald collecting plates and scurrying off to the kitchen.

"You, David, can help most by not breaking any of my grandmother's china. Stay where you are and have another piece of gingerbread."

"Only if you'll stay with me. I'm sure Karen can manage to wash a few teacups without your help."

A strange noise erupted from Mrs. J. I'd never heard it before, but I figured it had to be a laugh. It was higher pitched than her speaking voice, almost a giggle. But she never laughed, never mind giggled.

I listened, fascinated, to what she said next. "All right, I won't leave you alone, poor man." She was flirting!

Robin rolled his eyes. "Come on. Time to go." We replaced our slippers, shrugged into our coats, then headed out into the dusk.

I was about to say something about it being gross, his grandma being all coy with Mr. Allen, but Robin spoke first.

"I think they're cute," he said. "My dad was hysterical when Grandma starting dating, but Mr. Allen's been really good for her. Too bad he can't square dance anymore—arthritis. But neither can she with that cast on her leg, so it worked out all right."

"Cute?" I thought for a moment, searching for the right

thing to say. "Cute" wasn't a word I'd use about Mrs. J. Never. For a moment I debated between "gross" and "sweet" then decided against both words. "Whatever. I suppose it's companionship for them both."

"That's what Dad said after they'd been going out for few months."

"Really?" I couldn't think of anything else to add, so just listened while Robin chatted more about his plans for next year. Eventually he grew silent, too, and we were both quiet until we reached my place.

"Anything wrong?" he asked as he dropped me off.

"No," I lied. "I've just been thinking." About glasses.

"Okay, maybe we'll see each other again?"

"Sure, let me know if your grandmother needs help with another tea party."

"Oh . . . Goodbye, Darrah. It was nice meeting you."

"You too, Robin."

Mom was hanging around the front door, waiting for me, but I ignored her barrage of questions. "Got homework, Mom. Talk later."

In my room, I threw myself on my bed and tried to think. Glasses. Glasses and magnifiers. Lots and lots of them. All in the same drawer, right in the kitchen. She said she couldn't find them. But she knew where everything in her kitchen was, right down to which refrigerator shelf the lard was kept on; she must have known where her glasses were. Why did she lie?

"Darrah!" That was Andrew yelling from his room.

"What? I'm busy."

"Won't take a minute." Reluctantly I pushed off my bed and went down the hall.

He was sitting on the chair by his desk. "You're good at math, right?"

"No."

"Seriously?"

"Yes." I turned to leave the room.

"Darrah, what's the matter with you?"

"Nothing."

"Liar. I can see trouble on your face. Did that guy blow you off?"

"Who? Oh, Robin. No, actually he . . ." What had he said, something about seeing each other again? I'd been so wrapped up thinking about Mrs. J., I hadn't even noticed. If anything, I'd rejected him, not the other way around.

"Do you like him?"

"I don't know." I honestly hadn't thought about it. "All we talked about was TV shows and school. At her place, the old people did most of the talking. Anyway, it's none of your business. Why don't you ask Dad your question? I don't feel like facing math right now."

His face fell. "I hate asking Dad. He gives me a long lecture when I ask a simple question. All I want to know is—"

"Andrew, I don't want to think about math right now." Again, I turned to leave his room.

"You are in a bad mood."

I turned back. "I'm not."

"You are, too. What happened?"

So, I told him. I needed to talk to someone, and Andrew was there. I sat down on his bed and he straddled his chair, leaning over the back, facing me. Listening. Really listening, without interrupting. I told him how Mrs. J. wanted me to read newspapers to her, check recipes in cookbooks, measure and cook stuff. I told him how she kept saying she couldn't find her glasses and how I'd found them easily, not just glasses but magnifiers, lots of them.

"I know she exaggerates," I said, thinking about the way she let everyone think her arm was sprained when it wasn't. "But why would she lie? She's honest about everything else, or at least everything she's told me."

"You think?" Andrew said. "How do you know she isn't lying about everything?"

"She did lie at the circle, and that was serious, with the police there and everything."

"Really? What did she lie about?"

There was no way I was going to tell Andrew the true story of what happened at the hospital. "Nothing important, forget it."

"You want Super Geek to help figure this out? Why she hid her glasses and lied about them being lost?"

"Who?"

"Super Geek. That's me. I've been spending a lot of time

on the internet, no, not those places Mom and Dad are always going on about, just finding out stuff, like all the actors in *Star Trek* and what happened to them and—"

"Isn't that 'Trekkie' stuff, not 'geeky' stuff?"

"If you don't want me to help, I won't."

"How can you help?"

"Lack of computer time has fried your brain. Give me a few minutes." He turned back to the computer, keyed a few words into a search engine. "Does she throw up a lot?"

"What?"

"Vomiting, nausea, pain?"

"Of course she's in pain. Leg pain. She takes pills for it. I've never seen her throw up."

"Okay, that rules that out. Her eyes aren't pink and watery, are they?"

"No."

"How about headaches?"

"How am I supposed to know if she gets headaches? She never mentions them."

He went back to the search engine, reading, shaking his head, trying another site. I got up and went to look over his shoulder. I wasn't supposed to be using a computer except for school work, but I wasn't actually using it, Andrew was. I had figured out what he was doing.

"Change your keywords for the search." Andrew had typed in 'eye problems' and had come up with millions of hits. "Try 'loss of eyesight in the elderly' and search again."

"Elderly? You mean old?"

"Try elderly first. Or seniors. Or aging."

I watched as he keyed the words in. "Okay, got it, lots of medical sites about old people's eyes. 'The most common forms of eye disease in the elderly are cataracts and—'"

"Nope, cataracts can be fixed, Grandma had hers done. Mrs. J. would have had the surgery."

"Glauco . . . glaucoma. That's the one that sometimes has throwing up as a side effect. People have to use special drops in their eyes all the time."

"I haven't ever seen her barf or use drops."

"Maybe it's macu—"

"Macular degeneration," I read over his shoulder. "What's that? Move over, let me look." I half pulled him out of his chair, and scrolled down to the section on symptoms. "'Patients may complain of blurred or distorted vision, difficulty reading or driving, or increased reliance on brighter light, stronger glasses or magnifying lenses to perform tasks requiring fine visual acuity.' I bet that's it! She doesn't drive anymore, she has night lights everywhere and she leaves them on in the daytime, she cancelled all her newspapers, and there are all those magnifying glasses in the drawer."

"Is she going to go blind?"

I scanned down the page. "There are two kinds of macular degeneration, dry and wet."

"Yuck!"

I agreed with the "yuck" but that information didn't answer

Andrew's question. Or mine. "Doesn't matter. One kind messes up your eyes faster than the other. Listen to this: 'People with this disease have trouble discerning colors; specifically dark ones from dark ones and light ones from light ones.' Her pumpkin stairs! Orange edged in green. She can't see the edge of the steps. That's why they are painted in different colours! Here's something else that fits: 'Macular degeneration causes dark, blurred, or white areas in the centre of vision, so those afflicted with this disease use their side (peripheral) vision to see more clearly. Sometimes they appear not to be looking at the person they are speaking to, as they turn their head and use their peripheral vision to see better.'" I thought about Mrs. J. at the end of the circle, looking over my shoulder but talking to me. She was looking at me, the best way she could.

"Can I have my computer back now?" Andrew was bored, but I wasn't ready to quit.

"One minute more, okay?" I scrolled down until I found what I was looking for. He was hovering over my shoulder; I could feel his impatience growing. "Just a sec, I'll be done soon, promise."

I found what I was looking for and read it aloud. "Age-related macular degeneration (AMD) is a major cause of blindness in the elderly."

"So she is going to go blind? That's tough. Can I have my computer now?"

I read a bit more, then stopped. "Sure, thanks, Andy."

"Hey, it was fun."

Fun? Not for Mrs. J.

Back in my room I flopped on my bed, pulled my old teddy bear, Dixon, to my chest and hugged him hard. Suddenly, everything made sense. Even her comment to me at the end of the circle, "You'll figure it out," she had said.

I had figured out why she needed my help, and now I was depressed. She had been good to me, in her own way. She could be cranky, but she'd taught me about cooking and baking, which was fun although I hadn't expected it to be. I didn't want her to go blind. No one should ever be blind. It would be horrible not to be able to read, or watch TV, or see what you were eating, or how your hair looked, or if you had lettuce stuck in your teeth.

The last thing I read before surrendering Andrew's computer was about cures for the disease. "Today there is no known cure for macular degeneration, but scientists have hopes of finding a cure in the future."

That wouldn't help Mrs. J. She was old; she didn't have much future left.

For her, there would be no cure.

Chapter Ten

I SPENT MONDAY worrying about what I was going to say to
Mrs. Johnson when I saw her after school. Or if I was going
to say anything. Should I pretend I hadn't found her cache of
glasses? What was the point in telling her I knew? I still had to
spend more than thirty hours helping her before I'd finished
my sanctions, and she could make those hours miserable.
Sure, the potatoes had been dug up, so I wouldn't be freezing
my fingers in the garden, but what if she decided I had to
scrub the toilet or wash the kitchen floor? So far I'd escaped
doing any housework except washing up the cooking dishes,
and I wanted to keep it that way.

I took the bus. Mom had decided it was cheaper for me to use my student bus pass than for her to drive me to Mrs. J.'s twice a week. She'd whined about the price of gas, then hopped in the car to drive a few blocks to her gym! Typical Mom action.

I was on the bus when I came to a conclusion: I wouldn't mention the hidden glasses, or that I knew that Mrs. Johnson was going blind. There was no point.

So it was a bit of a shock when the first thing out of my mouth after "Hi, I'm here," was "I figured it out."

She didn't even ask me what I'd figured out. "I thought you might have," she said. "Looking for the tea strainer, you opened the wrong drawer, right?" She gestured at the teapot. "Help yourself, it's blueberry."

"Blueberries are supposed to be good for macular degeneration." I'd read that yesterday.

"Oh, you've even decided what's wrong with my eyes. How'd you do that?"

I poured myself some tea and slid onto the bench beside the table. "I asked Doctor Google."

"Of course. The computer."

I nodded, and didn't say anything for a while. "Why'd you lie about losing your glasses?" I finally blurted out.

She reached for the teapot and refilled her cup. This time I noticed how she looped a finger over the brim of her mug so she knew when the tea had reached the top, and she could stop pouring before it overflowed. We both sipped in silence.

"Glasses aren't doing me any good anymore," she said at last. "My eyes are getting worse."

"But I don't understand why you lied instead of just telling people you are going . . ." I caught myself before I finished the sentence.

She sighed. "I've lived in this house for nearly fifty years. My husband and I bought it before our children came, fixed it up, got the garden going. The house wasn't finished when we moved in; it needed a lot of work. We had tarpaper siding and windows made of plastic for the first while. But we finally got everything done and paid for." She ran a hand over the counter beside her. "My husband installed this new counter-top just before he got sick. One of the last things he did. Oh, how he missed being able to putter in the garden or down in the basement. But he got ill and . . ." She stopped and sighed again. "There are a lot of memories in this house. I don't want to leave them."

"Why would you have to leave?"

"Think, girl! A blind old lady living alone? Who's going to allow that? My sons would move me out of here and into one of those awful places faster than I could blink while their wives squabbled over who got grandma's hand-painted china."

"What places?"

"Those warehouses for old people. 'Care homes' they call them, but actually they are just places to store old folk until they die. Families call it 'doing the right thing.' I've seen it happen too many times, lost too many friends to those 'homes.' People move into a small room, away from their homes and gardens and the places they love. They sit down and start talking about how tired they are, then they grow quiet and then they die."

"But . . ." I stopped, not sure how to say what I wanted to say. That was the kind of place my Gran had gone to. But that really was the right thing to do. She couldn't remember to turn off the stove or the taps, and she kept running away. It was dangerous for her in her own home, even with a caregiver staying with her all the time.

"Spit it out, girl."

"It's not safe for you to be here alone."

"What's not safe? I know every inch of this house, every squeak in the floorboards, know where I have to be careful or I'll bump into the sideboard, know where the glasses are when I need water in the middle of the night. My brain is working well. I don't forget to eat or go to bed or flush the toilet."

"But . . ."

"No more discussion. This house is part of me. I'm not leaving it except in a pine box."

"Box?"

She glared at me, and I got it, a bit late. Box. Coffin. She was talking about dying here, right here in her home. I shivered. Someone must be walking over my grave, that's what my dad says when you get shivers and you aren't cold.

"Karen comes over every day, she does the laundry, the cleaning, helps me with meals. My family thinks she's just a friend, and she is, but I pay her well for her time. I need her. They don't know how much."

"You need me, too," I said softly.

"Piffle. I can manage fine without you, girl. But when I found out that you could act, I thought hearing you read to me would be entertaining. David reads in a monotone, and Karen doesn't like reading aloud."

"You don't have papers anymore." I looked down at the bench which used to hold a stack of newspapers.

"Wasn't getting through them, so I cancelled my subscriptions. Told you that. Get my news on the radio."

I sat for a moment, thinking. "Who knows?" I asked.

"I'm pretty sure you don't mean who knows that I cancelled my newspaper subscriptions?"

I shook my head. "No."

"Karen, David. And now you. No one else except my doctor."

I thought for a moment. I could bargain with her, promise not to tell anyone about her going blind if she'd cancel the rest of my sanction hours.

"I will, if that's what you want."

"I didn't say anything!"

"Your silence spoke for you. You were thinking of blackmailing me."

"No, I wasn't."

"Yes, you were."

"No, I . . . Okay, I did think that, but just for a minute. I want to finish my sanctions. Besides, my parents would make me."

"I am sure they would."

"I won't tell anyone, Mrs. J., I promise."

She laughed, a deeper laugh than the one I'd heard yesterday. "I know you won't, girl. You're too honest, in spite of not wanting to be. I'll wager you would have turned yourself in for pulling that fire alarm if they hadn't caught you first."

"I would not—"

"Yes, you would have. You have a kind heart, even though you fight it."

"Kind heart?" No one had ever said that about me. I wasn't sure I liked being thought of as a marshmallow.

The phone rang and she grabbed it without looking. She was right. She knew exactly where everything in the house was. "Call me later," she said into the phone, not even saying "hello" first. I could hear a man's voice crackling over the receiver, but couldn't make out the words. Mrs. J. turned her head away from me. "That test outcome is no surprise," she said, her voice lower, then listened again. "All right, all right, I promise. I'll come in tomorrow. You can talk all you want, but I refuse to . . ." She replaced the phone in its base, without finishing her sentence or saying goodbye.

"Damned doctor's also trying to blackmail me." She pushed herself up from the stool and grabbed her cane. "I promised him I'd lie down every afternoon for an hour. Didn't do it earlier, so guess I have to now. Whip up a batch of cheese biscuits, and knock on the bedroom door before you leave. Mind you wash your dishes, a good cook always—"

"—cleans up after herself." I finished the familiar sentence for her. She nodded, poured herself a glass of water and swallowed a pill from the bottle she kept in a kitchen cupboard. I watched her move slowly down the hall, one hand on the wall, the other on her cane. She didn't look back, and the bedroom door clicked firmly shut behind her.

The biscuits were all mixed, dry and liquid ingredients together and just the right texture, when the thought hit me: Mrs. J. looked old today. Old and tired. My eyes misted over, and I sniffed back tears. "Everyone gets old. Snap out of it, girl." Sheesh. Now I was sounding like her in my own head. I dumped the dough onto the floured counter and began kneading it more vigorously than the instructions called for or was good for the biscuits. "Whatever," I said out loud, pounding my fist into the dough. "Whatever."

"What did that poor dough do to you to deserve that rough treatment?" someone asked.

I jumped. "Robin! How did you get here?"

"No one answered when I knocked, so I just came in. Gran never locks her door. Where is she?"

"She's having a nap."

"A what?"

"Nap. You know. Lie down, put your head on a pillow, rest.

Pass me a glass from that cupboard." I liked using a heavy tumbler to cut the dough, even though I now knew where the cookie cutters were kept and could have used those to shape the biscuits.

"Of course I know what a nap is, I only look dense. Actually I'm quite smart."

"Really?"

"Really. But why is Gran lying down in the middle of the afternoon?"

"Her doct . . . uh . . . her leg hurt."

"I'm not surprised. Yesterday I had to take her to the doctor and he prescribed more of those pain pills she uses. I promised her I'd pick them up today. She started complaining that her leg hurt as soon as he took the cast off."

"Her cast isn't off. She's still wearing it."

"That's a different one. Didn't you notice? It has straps and can be removed. It's got balloons inside . . ."

"Balloons?"

He shrugged. "Something like that. The doctor called it an air boot. Probably not really balloons."

He disappeared into the front hall and returned pushing a three-wheeled walker with black rubber handles and hand brakes like a bicycle. An old-fashioned wire basket was hooked onto the front.

"Looks like a tricycle. Hey, it even has a bicycle bell." I reached a floury hand and made the shiny little bell ding. "Sounds the same as the one I had on my tricycle."

"Don't let Gran hear you say that! She snarled at the doctor when he suggested it, said she'd never use one of those things."

"So why did you bring her one? And where did you get it?"

"The doctor called Mom and told her to make sure Gran got herself a walker. Said she needed more support than her cane until her leg muscles got stronger, so Mom sent me to the hospital to pick one up. They have a basement room full of crutches, walkers, those plastic seats for the toilet and other stuff that they lend out. Took me forever to get down to the basement and then come back up. Those elevators are really slow."

Okay, let's fast forward over any slow hospital elevator references. "You're taking a chance bringing it here. She'll explode when she sees it."

"She will, won't she? I forgot, I have to go. You can introduce Gran to the walker. Bye." But he sat down on the tall wooden stool and grinned instead of heading for the front door.

"I bet you won't go anywhere until you have some biscuits." I popped the tray into the preheated oven and set the timer.

Robin held up a finger and smiled. "Option One, eat and get bawled out by Gran." He held up another finger. "Or, Option Two, leave, escape getting reamed out and stay hungry. That's a hard decision."

I turned away, quickly. He looked like one of those Roman

gods, blond curly hair, tall. I hadn't noticed it before, but he was—

"What's a hard decision, Robin?"

Mrs. J. had come down the hallway so quietly neither of us had heard her. "What decision do you—get that damned thing out of here. Now!" She had seen the walker.

Robin looked at me. "How soon will those biscuits be ready? Can I have one to go?"

"You're not going anywhere, young man, until you explain why you brought that thing into my house. I told the doctor that I didn't want it. You heard me!"

"The doctor called Mom," said Robin. "He said he didn't think you paid any attention to him. Mom told me to go get it. It's not my fault. I got your prescription, too." He held out a small white bag from the pharmacy. "I remembered to pick these up."

"No point trying to get on my good side," she said. "You heard me tell the doctor I wouldn't use an old fart's walker!"

Old fart? She was annoyed. I thought I'd try to settle her down. "You don't have to use the walker all the time, Mrs. J."

"That's not what the doctor told her," said Robin.

"Hey, I'm trying to help you out," I hissed at him.

"I don't care what the doctor said. I hate that damned thing."

"You haven't tried it yet, Gran. Maybe it will be fun."

"If the snow holds off, we can go for walks while I'm here. It might be handy for outside. Just for a while. Until you get stronger, you know, um . . ." My voice trailed off; it sort of withered away under her stare, my words drying up.

She glared at me some more, then at Robin again. "Conspiracy!"

We didn't say anything, and she pointed her cane at Robin perched on the stool. "Go sit somewhere else, you know that's my place. But first, wheel that thing out of my sight. And you, girl, put on the kettle. I need tea." I scurried around moving the bowls and rolling pin off the counter, wiping it down and filling the kettle.

"I thought you were taking a nap, Mrs. J. It hasn't been an hour yet."

"Got bored."

"I bet you couldn't stand leaving Darrah alone in your kitchen. Afraid she'd break something." Robin was back, without the walker.

Both Mrs. J. and I glared at him. "I've never broken . . ."

"Nonsense, the girl's quite capable of . . ."

"Hey, that's not fair, both of you picking on me at once."

"Shall we let him stay until the biscuits are ready? Or shall we evict him now?" Mrs. J. flourished her cane and looked ready to personally toss Robin out. I had a vision of her grabbing him by the scruff of his neck and throwing him out the front door, like a burly club bouncer.

"Hey," he protested again. "It was a joke, enough already."

I picked up the rolling pin. "I think he should leave," I said, taking a step towards him and hoping I looked as scary Mrs. J. did.

"The kettle's boiling, it needs you," Robin said, grinning at me. "And by the way, Gran does the scowl way better than you."

"Had more years to practice," said his grandmother. "How are those biscuits coming?"

The timer dinged. I checked, declared the biscuits ready and pulled them out of the oven, carefully leaving the oven door ajar ("no point in wasting all that heat") as Mrs. J. always instructed. Robin grabbed a biscuit right off the pan.

"Ow, they're hot," he muttered through the first bite.

"Where are your manners, young man? You know better than to talk with your mouth full. I've had enough of you today. Go away. Take the girl with you."

"What about your tea?" I asked.

"Make a pot, then go. It's early, you can have credit for the full two and a half hours. I've had enough company for now."

"What about a good cook always cleaning up after herself?"

"You're excused for today, girl. Karen's coming over later to unstrap this contraption and help me do the ridiculous exercises the doctor wants me to do. Don't see any use to them, but he's insisting. She'll clean up. You two get yourselves out of here."

"She's cranky today," said Robin once we were in the car.

"Really? I hadn't noticed."

He ignored my sarcasm. "The doctor told her she'd have lots of physiotherapy and would have to do exercises every day."

"Exercises? Like a treadmill? Or swimming?" I had a bizarre vision of Mrs. J. in a pink flowered bathing cap doing lengths in the community pool.

"No, easier ones. Like drawing letters of the alphabet with her big toe. I guess she'll graduate to something harder later on. Hey, do you . . ."

"I thought she'd be in a cast longer."

"It wasn't really a break, just a crack in a leg bone."

"The tibia?" I asked. "That's what Andrew broke when he was seven."

"No, the other bone, the one that isn't so big or important. I think the doctor just put the cast on to slow her down so she couldn't dig up her garden or do something else that would make it snap right through."

I was still thinking of the pink bathing cap. "I can't imagine her swimming."

"Nope, I can't either. But in the spring, she'll get lots of exercise. She likes to mow the lawn herself, with one of those old push mowers. Hey, you want to . . ."

"Want to what? Help your grandmother draw letters with her big toe? Not a chance."

"No, she won't let anyone but Karen help her. I meant would you like to . . . there's this new movie, aliens conquering earth, I thought . . ."

"I've heard of it. It's a remake of a classic, isn't it? Got good reviews."

"Would you like to go?"

"With you?" Was he . . . he was asking me out! I felt my cheeks go red, and turned away from him, staring out the car window. Of course I'd like to go out with him, but I had this awkward problem with my parents.

"No, with Gran. Of course with me. Who did you think I meant?"

"I'd like to, but I have to ask my parents."

"If they say yes, will you go?"

I turned away from the window, but couldn't look him in the eyes, so I stared down at my hands. "I don't think they'll let me."

"What? They want to see my references?"

"No, it isn't that."

"What is it then?"

Might as well get it over with. "I'm grounded."

"You? What did you do, rob a bank?"

I wanted to tell him, but I couldn't. How could I say it?— I'm sorry Robin but I'm the reason your grandmother's got a broken leg. I'm the reason you have to take her to doctors' appointments, dig up her garden and pick up her prescriptions and walkers. That's why I'm grounded.

"I can't tell you," I said at last. "But I'm really, really sorry." Consequence Number Three was still hanging over my life like a black cloud. I was grounded until all the sanctions were finished, until I no longer had to go to Mrs. J.'s twice a week.

We stopped in front of my house. "When are you ungrounded?"

I did a quick calculation of my remaining hours. "After New Year's."

"That's a long time. Maybe you did rob a bank."

"No, I didn't. Almost as bad, but I can't tell you. I'm so sorry, Robin." I opened the car door and escaped before he could ask what I was so sorry for and why I was crying.

Chapter Eleven

I DIDN'T MAKE IT into the house. The front door flew open and Andrew ran out. "Hey, who's the guy? Thought you were grounded. Does Dad know you're on a date with a guy?"

"It's not a date! He just drove me home." I tried to push past Andrew but he didn't move. He made a noise, almost a grunt and then he fell. It was as if his body had forgotten how to hold itself upright. He fell straight back, as if he were a knocked-over tin soldier.

Andrew's head hit the lawn, but the rest of him landed on the cement sidewalk. "Mom," I yelled, kneeling down beside my brother. "Mom!"

But Robin was there first. He hadn't driven off, he had been watching. "What's wrong with him?" he asked. "Should I call 911?"

"Quick, put your jacket under his head in case he bangs his head around. Mom! Mom!"

She was suddenly beside me. "Oh, Darrah, oh, Andrew, oh . . ."

"Stay calm, Mom. He's going to be okay. One of Andrew's arms had flown up, narrowly missing Robin's face. "Move his backpack out of the way, Robin, so he doesn't bang against it, and you move too."

Robin stepped back. "Shouldn't we call 911?" He already had his phone out.

"Yes. Call them, call!"

"No, Mom, no! You know what the doctors keep telling you. Let the seizure take its course. Wait at least five minutes."

It didn't last five minutes, it didn't even last three. I was counting the seconds, as I always did if I couldn't see a clock. Usually Andrew's seizures were only a minute or two, but it always seemed like forever while it was happening. "One hundred and thirty-five," I said out loud. "One hundred and thirty-six . . . thirty-seven." He stopped jerking, his eyelids stopped flickering up and down and he began to breathe normally again. It was over.

"Help me get him into the house," said Mom, reaching under his legs.

"I can do it," said Robin. "You get the door and tell me

where to take him." He scooped Andrew up, lifting him easily. Mom flew up the stairs, and held the door open. I could hear her voice directing Robin. "Up the stairs, first right, be careful, don't drop him."

I picked up my backpack and shut the driver's door of Robin's car. He'd left it open when he jumped out to help us. I shut the front door behind me. Mom had left that wide open, too. I dumped my backpack in the front hall and started up the stairs.

Robin was on his way down. "Your mom says he'll be fine now, that he just needs to sleep for a bit. She's staying up there with him. Are you okay?"

"Yes," I said, then burst into tears. "Andrew hasn't had a seizure for at least two weeks. We thought his new medication was working."

"Need a hug?" He put his arms around me and pulled me to him without waiting for my answer.

I bawled louder. Yes, I needed a hug. I needed more than one, I needed a whole barrel of hugs. It was too much. Too much for Mom and Dad and too much for me. Andrew looked so helpless during a seizure—we were helpless. Then he would be pale and tired for hours, for days afterwards. "It's not fair," I said into Robin's shoulder. "He's not even twelve." I cried some more.

"Um, my jacket's getting soggy." Robin steered me to the kitchen and sat me down on a chair. He looked around, found the box of tissue on top of the fridge and held it out to me. "Here, mop up. But I've still got one dry shoulder. You're welcome to it if you need it."

"I'll be okay. Thanks for the tissue." And the hug, I thought. Especially for the hug.

"Want to talk about it?"

Did I? I must have needed to talk, because it all came flooding out: how our lives had changed so much since Andrew's seizures started; how we were always on edge, waiting for the next one; how I didn't get the part in the play because Mom took him to the hospital; how I got so mad I . . .

Then I stopped. Even while my mouth was running overtime and my eyes were pumping out the tears they'd been saving up for months, I knew I couldn't say anymore.

"It's been rough, hasn't it?"

I nodded, still not trusting my mouth not to blurt out things it shouldn't.

There was a cough from the hallway. Mom was behind us. "Sorry to interrupt," she said to Robin, "but whoever you are, I want to thank you for your help."

"You're welcome, ma'am."

Then she turned to me. "Darrah, you're supposed to be doing your sanctions with Mrs. Johnson. Why are you here?"

Robin and I spoke at once. "Mom, he was driving me . . ."

"My grandmother asked me to take . . ."

"You're Mrs. Johnson's grandson?"

"Yes, ma'am. She asked me to bring Darrah home."

"She did?"

"Yes, ma'am. Gran sent her away early today."

"Oh."

Thankfully the word "sanctions" didn't ring any bells for Robin. "I wouldn't skip out on my hours, Mom," I said indignantly.

"I know you wouldn't, Darrah. I wasn't thinking straight." She turned to Robin. "I'm sorry, young man . . ."

"Robin," I said. "His name is Robin, Mom."

"I'm sorry I leaped to conclusions, Robin, and thank you for your help. I'm afraid I always get a bit emotional after one of Andrew's . . ." Then she burst into tears.

Robin grabbed a handful of tissues from the box he was still holding and passed them to Mom. For a minute I thought he was going to offer her a hug, too, but all he did was pat her awkwardly on the shoulder.

She grabbed the tissues, muttered "thanks," and fled.

"Is she all right?" Robin asked.

I nodded. "She'll be okay. We all will. I guess we all thought —hoped—that the new meds would stop the seizures completely. I think that's why she's so upset."

"I don't blame her. Need another hug?"

"No. Stay away or I'll start bawling again."

"Are you sure I can't help?"

"No, thanks, no one can help. Andrew will sleep, Mom will helicopter around him when he wakes up, and for the next week or so Dad will invent six more ways of not saying 'epilepsy' and life in the Patrick household will go on."

"I'm so sorry, Darrah. Listen, promise me you'll let me know if I can do anything?"

I was pretty sure there wasn't anything he could do that would help me or Andrew or anyone, but said, "Sure. Now please go away, there's nothing more you can do here. I've got to check on Andrew. And Mom."

"Okay, but call if you need to use my other shoulder, okay?"

"I will," I said, and meant it. "Thank you. Thank you for everything."

He let himself out. As the door clicked shut behind him, I sighed. "Welcome to my world, Robin."

The house was silent, so I tiptoed up the stairs.

Mom was lying down on the bed beside Andrew. It looked as if they were both asleep. I didn't disturb them and instead went back downstairs, wondering what I could find for supper.

In the fridge was half of the barbecued chicken Mom had brought home two days ago. All that was left was one leg, one wing and some bits of meat sticking to the rest of the bones. Not enough for dinner. Maybe I could turn it into soup? I pulled as much meat as I could off the bones, then broke the carcass into smaller pieces and tossed them in a pot of water. Barbecued chicken might make interesting soup stock. Once the stock had simmered for a while I would take out all the bones, let them cool, then remove the rest of the meat from them before putting it back in the soup. That would be less greasy than taking the meat off the chicken legs to make soup for Mrs. J.

So, would I make chicken noodle or chicken rice? There weren't any noodles in the house except in a box of Kraft dinner but there was a bag of rice. Okay, barbecued chicken with rice soup coming up.

I thought back to the soup recipe in *Foods, Nutrition and Home Management* and dug around in the refrigerator crisper. All it yielded was half a tired onion, three soft tomatoes and several small baggies of equally tired small, peeled carrots— lunch snacks that Andrew had brought home untouched. While I was rummaging in the crisper, I tossed out two apples with soggy black spots and an orange that smelled funny. Maybe there were vegetables in the freezer? I checked. Frozen mini-pizzas, burritos, a heat-and-serve lasagna. Fries, curly and straight, not good for soup. But there were frozen peas and an almost empty bag of kernel corn. Hiding in the back of the freezer was something that might have once been ice cream, sitting uncovered in a bowl. I put that in the sink to thaw, rinsed the ice crystals off the peas and corn and put them in a bowl with the chicken meat to add to the soup later.

When Dad got home the onion was browning while the chicken bones cooled. "You're cooking?" he said, surprised. "Where's your Mom?"

"Upstairs. Andrew had another—"

He was gone before I finished the sentence; I could hear

his feet pounding up the stairs. I scooped the onions into the soup stock, and went to work on the carrots.

Although I'd baked biscuits once already today, I thought that Andrew would like them, so I dug out the flour and baking powder I'd had Mom buy and started mixing. I now knew the recipe by heart, and it was somehow comforting to be kneading dough while the soup simmered. It was already smelling good.

By the time Mom, Dad and Andrew came downstairs, the soup was ready, the biscuits cooling on a rack, and the table was set.

Mom looked even more surprised than Dad had. "I was going to order Chinese," she said.

"No need to."

"Biscuits?" said Andrew. His voice was weak, but he wasn't as pale as he often was after a seizure.

"Yes, sorry, just plain ones. There was only a bit of cheese and it was mouldy so I threw it out." We did have some processed cheese slices, but I didn't think they would work in biscuits. How could anyone grate those floppy squares?

Andrew was already eating. "Good anyway," was what I thought he said through the mouthful of biscuits.

Dad asked for a second helping of soup. Andrew almost finished his bowl and ate three biscuits. Mom kept staring at me as if I'd just flown in from outer space.

"Mom, what's wrong?"

"You made dinner."

week. I'm just learning, but I don't mind trying."

Mom burst into tears again. "Oh, Darrah, oh, Darrah, oh, Darrah."

"Oh, Mom, don't do that. It's no big deal." But it was a big deal. That was the first time in months that Mom had oh-Darrahed me because she was proud of something I'd done, not ashamed, and not because she was upset with me.

"It's no big deal," I repeated. "Stop crying, Mom."

Dad smiled. "I'm sure we can work out a satisfactory raise in your allowance if you take on more household responsibility."

Wow, I wasn't expecting that one. But maybe there was a catch. "Only cooking, okay? I'm not going to push that heavy vacuum around, and no cleaning toilets! Yuck!"

Mom stood up, came over and hugged me. "Cooking is more than enough, Darrah. The vacuum and I are on good terms, and I don't mind doing the other housework. You just cook."

"It's a deal," I said.

"Good. Since you made dinner tonight, I'll clean up. You and Andrew go upstairs and do your homework. Take your laptop, Darrah. I think we can forget that consequence."

She'd lifted Consequence Number Two! That barbecued chicken rice soup must be magical. I made a mental note to write down the recipe before I forgot it.

Consequence Number One, using my phone, had ended after the circle—I think Mom couldn't stand not being able

"So?"

"I didn't ask you. You did it on your own."

"You were sleeping beside Andrew," I said. "I tho
try to cook something. But you need to go grocery sh
there's no fruit left."

"I was going to do that this afternoon."

"How about I help make the list? I can tell you th
need to make stew like I did at Mrs. Johnson's. I didn
eat any of it, but it smelled good. I wouldn't mind
some at home."

Mom nodded, and Dad put down his spoon. "Tha
Darrah," he said seriously. "You stepped in when y
needed."

"Brownies?" said Andrew. "Can you make brownie
brownies. With sprinkles. And lots of chocolate icing.

"Probably. I'll ask Mrs. J. if she has a good rec
brownies. It would be fun to make them."

Mom finally said something. "You like cooking? I h

"You don't like cooking?" said my father, surprised.
never told me that."

Mom shrugged. "What could I say? Announce 'I'm
cook and I hate doing it' and hire a chef?"

"Don't need to hire anyone," said Andrew. "Darr
cook for us."

"Would you?" asked Mom.

"Could you?" asked Dad.

"I . . . I . . . yes, I think I can. Maybe a couple of din

to call me any time she wanted to. Only Consequence Number Three was left. Grounding. "Maybe I could . . ." I started, then thought better of it. Once I produced some great dinners, it would be a better time to ask about going out with Robin. For now, I'd stay quiet and earn some more parental appreciation.

"That's okay, Mom. I can clean up. Why don't you and Andrew clear the table and I'll do the rest?"

The look on Mom's face made me wish I'd been more sincere about my offer, not just angling for good behaviour points.

"I'll help," said Dad, and he was beaming, too, smiling as if I'd just ridden my new two-wheeler down the sidewalk by myself.

My parents being so grateful was almost harder to take than their being angry at me. I picked up two soup bowls and scurried into the kitchen where no one could see my face. All this gratitude—I had a horrible suspicion I was blushing.

Chapter Twelve

I CHECKED OUT BROWNIE recipes on the internet, but decided not to try to make them until I'd asked Mrs. J. Maybe she had a special never-fail recipe, or maybe the red book had some tips. I wouldn't mind a good recipe for chocolate chip cookies, either. Mom sometimes made the kind of cookies where the dough is already mixed and frozen in a big pail and you just thaw, scoop and bake. I bet I could learn to make cookies from scratch.

When I arrived at Mrs. J.'s on Wednesday, I grabbed slippers in a hurry, then headed into the kitchen. She wasn't there, waiting for me, her tea sitting beside her.

"Mrs. J? It's me." No answer. I called again. "Mrs. J?"

"Who is it?" Her voice came from down the hall, maybe from her bedroom. She wasn't in the bathroom. That door was open.

"It's me, Darrah."

"Is it that time already? I'll be right there." While I waited for her, I looked for the red *Foods, Nutrition and Home Management* book, hoping to find a recipe for brownies, but the book wasn't on the kitchen table. Nothing was on the table except two prescription bottles of pills. I picked one up. "Take one or two every four hours for pain." That bottle was almost empty, but the second bottle was full, even had the fluffy cotton stuffed into the top. Don't know why drugstores stick that cotton on top of the pills. Maybe so they don't rattle around? Or maybe it's some sort of pharmacists' rule?

I heard her cane thump on the floor, then Mrs. J. came down the hall from her bedroom. She moved slowly, and held on to the counter as she edged her way around to her usual seat. "Put the kettle on, girl. I need tea." She wasn't wearing the air boot today, just using her cane.

I filled the kettle, turned it on, then rummaged in the cupboard for her blueberry tea. There wasn't any. "What kind of tea would you like? The blueberry stuff's all gone."

"Doesn't matter, just something hot." She groaned as she hitched herself up on the stool. "Put those away," she said, gesturing at the pills. "Damn things make me nauseous."

My own stomach lurched as I realized that her pain was my fault. I didn't say anything except: "Where do you want me to put the pills?"

"Second shelf, by the tea."

I started to do as she asked, but she stopped me. "No, changed my mind. Pass me a glass of water and one of them before you put them away."

"Are you hurting?" What a stupid question to ask. Why would she ask for a pain pill if she felt fine. "I'm so sorry your leg's still sore, Mrs. J. I'm really sorry."

I put the glass of water and one pill, the second last one in the nearly empty container, in front of her. She put it in her mouth, grimaced, swallowed, then grimaced again. "Forget it. What do you want to do today?"

"Make brownies."

"Brownies?"

"With sprinkles."

"Don't have any sprinkles. Besides, good, moist brownies aren't as easy to make as most people think."

"Oh." Disappointed, I poured out the warming water from the teapot, and added boiling water and a scoop of tea called "Constant Comment." I knew she liked this one, it smelled of oranges and other spices, as well as tea. "My brother asked for brownies. He had a seizure last night and I thought—"

"He has epilepsy, doesn't he? He's the reason you were at the hospital the same day I was there. Is he all right?"

"He will be," I said, taking the tea strainer out of the drawer. "But Mom gets upset when he has a seizure." Then, perhaps to change the subject, I announced, "I made dinner last night, soup from a left-over barbecued chicken, and I baked biscuits, too."

She nodded. "I thought you'd be a good cook. You're clever, and a cook has to be inventive. Takeout barbecued chicken carcass for stock? Never thought of that."

"It was a success; everyone liked it. Now I'm going to cook two dinners a week for the family, and get a raise in my allowance."

"Good." She tried to pick up the teapot, then let it thump back onto the counter. "You filled it too full. Come over here and pour my tea. The pot's too heavy."

I'd only filled it halfway, but I did as she asked. "So you don't think I'm ready for brownies?"

She held the mug to her lips, blew across the tea and sighed. "No, you probably could manage them fine. I'm too tired today to help you."

"Is something wrong with your leg? Shouldn't it be getting better by now? It's been weeks since . . ."

"Don't want to talk about it."

"Sorry, I just . . ."

"Wacky Cake, that's what we'll make."

"Wacky Cake?"

"It's all mixed in one pan, the one you bake it in, then you serve it from the same pan. It's fast, easy and fail-proof. An old recipe of my mother's. Grab my recipes, there, on top of the fridge."

Her recipes were in a small box, written out on file cards, the kind I use to make cue cards when I'm trying to learn lines for a play. The box smelled musty and the headings on the section dividers were written in faded ink. I peered at

them—"Soups," "Salad Dressings," "Breads," "Desserts"—
and decided to look in "Cakes and Cookies." Logical. There it
was, a pale blue card labelled "Wacky Cake." In spidery writing, the same writing as the recipe, beside a smudge of what
looked like chocolate, was a date: September 20, 193_. The
smudge covered the last number. Underneath that was a note
"Janie made this by herself today." Janie? Oh, Mrs. Johnson!
This recipe card must have belonged to Mrs. J.'s mother!

The old lady in the kitchen vanished, and I saw instead a
small girl with long pigtails and a flour smudge on her nose.

"Find the recipe?" The pigtails were gone; Mrs. J., grey hair,
cane and all, was back.

"What? Oh, yes, I found it." I scanned the ingredients.
"Vinegar? What kind of a cake has vinegar in it?"

"This one," she said curtly, and then the phone rang.

She grabbed it, grunted "hello," then listened. Finally she
said, "No, no need to do that. Drop the boy off here. I'll get
Robin to drive him home later. Go do what you have to do,
he'll be fine."

She grunted a few more times then, with a final "you're
welcome," she hung up the phone. I was only half listening,
still checking the Wacky Cake recipe. "Who's Robin driving
home?" I asked.

"You. And your brother."

"Andrew? Andrew's coming here?" I dropped the file card.
"Why?" I asked, scrambling to pick it up.

"There's an emergency at your mother's office. She has to
go help out, right away, something that has to be dealt with

immediately or dire consequences will befall the whole company. Your father's in an important meeting; it's going to run late and he can't get away to look after your brother. Or to pick you up. She doesn't want to leave your brother alone."

"She always watches him carefully after a seizure," I said, thinking of how Mom hovered around Andrew until he blew up and told her to leave him alone, to stop helicoptering.

"Your mom said she would come and get you and take you home so you could keep an eye on your brother. I told her to bring him to you instead. You can watch out for him here just as well as at your house."

"Here?" My brain wasn't absorbing what she'd said. "Andrew's coming to your house?"

"That's what I said. While you're making sure he takes off his shoes and puts on slippers, you might want to look at your own feet. You're multicolored this afternoon."

She was right. I was wearing one purple and one orange slipper. "I was thinking about brownies; wasn't paying attention."

"I know the feeling very well. People say you're forgetting things, but what you are really doing is not focusing on the right thing at the right time."

"You don't forget things, Mrs. J. You know where everything in this kitchen is. Bet you know where everything in the whole house is kept."

"Told you, girl. It's my house. I know it and it knows me. The only way anyone will get me out of here is—"

"Don't say that!"

"Interrupting is very rude, girl."

"I'm sorry, but I know what you were going to say and it gives me the creeps. I don't want to hear it. Please." I shivered and wished that whoever was walking where my grave would be some day would go walk somewhere else.

"You have a point. It is a rather 'creepy' statement. I won't say it again."

"Thanks." I looked at the recipe for Wacky Cake. "I bet you know this one by heart. You've been making it since you were, how old?"

"I can't remember how old I was when I first made it, but I had to stand on a chair to reach the sugar in the cupboard. Mother was out and I decided to bake a cake to surprise her. I think I got the bigger surprise, a good spanking when my father got home."

"Your father beat you?"

"They called it discipline back then, not abuse. But yes, he did. With the back of a hairbrush. On my behind."

"Why? You were doing something good."

"I wasn't allowed to use the stove by myself."

"Did you have to light a fire? Was it one of those wood stoves?"

"No, it was a brand new electric stove. All gleaming white. My mother kept telling me how easy it was to use, so I thought I'd try." She winced, as if the spanking she had received so many decades ago still stung.

"Get the square glass baking pan, and let's get started. No

bowls to wash up; everything is mixed in that one pan."

I had my head in the low cupboard where the baking dishes were kept when the doorbell rang.

"Ouch!" Even though I knew Mom was coming, I'd still jumped at the sound, banging my head against the top of the cupboard. "I'll get it," I said, needlessly as Mrs. J. made no attempt to move from her perch.

Mom told me to make sure Andrew did his homework and keep an eye on him, reminded him to mind his manners, and said she was sorry she couldn't come in and say "hello" to Mrs. Johnson but she had to dash.

"Why are your feet two different colours? What are those things anyway?" asked Andrew.

I pulled off the purple slipper and tossed it into the basket, found the other orange one and pulled it on. "Slippers. Grab a pair," I said.

"I'll just wear my socks."

"No you won't. House rules: no outside shoes, no bare feet or socks."

"They're all wimp colours," he complained, surveying the slippers. "Except the orange ones. Can I wear those?"

"No. Hang up your coat and backpack, take off your shoes. Once you're ready, bring your homework and come to the kitchen. I'm working."

I'd measured the flour, cocoa and sugar into the pan by the time Andrew came in. He'd taken his time, probably agonizing over which pair of slippers to wear. On his feet were brown ones with thin yellow stripes. They must have been at the bottom of the basket as I hadn't noticed them before, and they were much too big for him.

"Mrs. Johnson, this is my brother, Andrew."

"How do you do, Andrew?"

"Fine. What's Darrah making?"

"Wacky Cake."

"What kind?"

"Chocolate cake," I said. "Sit down on the bench and start your homework."

"No, come sit by me, boy. I'd like to see what passes for homework these days. What grade are you in?"

"Five." He'd pulled up the other tall stool, the one that was usually pushed into a corner, and the two of them sat side by side. Andrew wriggled uncomfortably.

"What's your arithmetic homework?" Mrs. J. asked.

He looked puzzled.

"Math," I explained.

Andrew put his math text on the counter. "I've got lots. It's review. Fifty questions by tomorrow."

The two of them bent their heads over Andrew's math homework. I continued with the Wacky Cake, making three holes in the dry ingredients, putting the vinegar, the vanilla and the oil each in a different hole.

"DO NOT BEAT" the recipe insisted in capital letters, underlined, so I mixed well "with a fork" as instructed, and popped the cake into the oven (preheated to 350 degrees).

Andrew was reading the questions to Mrs. J., and she was

figuring out the answers in her head. They were racing to see who could get the answer first. I could tell Mrs. J. beat Andrew almost every time—she nodded her head just a bit and almost smiled when she got it—but she usually let him say the answer before she did.

Once again, Robin appeared in the kitchen unannounced. "Hi Gran, hi kid, how you feeling?"

"I'm feeling fine," I answered, even though I knew he was talking to Andrew. "I think you have nasal radar that can smell something baking from miles away."

He smiled. He had a wonderful smile.

"Bet that's Wacky Cake."

"How'd you know?"

"Gran used to let me make it when I was little."

"Good, then why don't you make the icing?"

He laughed and reached for the recipe card. "Okay, if I can use this cheat sheet. It's been awhile."

I could smell the chocolate cake baking. Andrew and Mrs. J. said an answer at the same time and laughed. Robin whistled as he blended butter and sugar together in a small pot. Outside, it was dark and cold, but in here it was warm and bright. I could see my reflection in the bay window; the overhead lights reflecting back from the dark.

I sat on the bench in the kitchen nook and watched and listened and felt warm. Not warm from the oven heat, but inside. At first I didn't recognize that feeling. Then I realized what it was.

I was happy.

The four of us finished the cake. Mrs. J. had a small piece and pronounced it "acceptable," except the icing was too sweet. Andrew asked her if we could borrow the recipe. Maybe he could help me make it at home.

I promised to take good care of the recipe card and return it the next time, then slipped it into Andrew's math book. "I'll let you help if you copy it out for me," I told him.

"Deal."

"It's after five," said Robin. "Isn't your dad coming for you, Darrah?"

"No," said Andrew. "You're driving us home."

"Meant to ask you, forgot, sorry," said Mrs. J.

"No problem." Robin smiled at me. "Always a pleasure."

The warm happy feeling stayed with me all the way home. Andrew leaned over the back seat and chattered at Robin who kept turning and smiling at me.

The warm happy feeling was still with me when we stopped outside our house.

"Thanks for the ride," I said.

"Yeah, thanks," said Andrew, climbing out of the backseat. "I like your grandma," he told Robin cheerfully.

Then it happened, and the warm feeling twisted in my stomach and turned into something cold and frightening, as Andrew continued, "Too bad she's going blind."

Chapter Thirteen

ANDREW DIDN'T REALIZE what he'd said, but Robin understood immediately. He stared at me for a long, long moment,
reached across the empty front seat, pulled the passenger
door shut then drove off, leaving me standing on the sidewalk. All without a word.

Andrew was in the front hall. He hadn't even taken off his
coat when I grabbed his shoulders and started shaking him.
Shake. "You stupid idiot!" *Shake, shake.* "Now Robin knows."
Shake. "He'll tell his parents."

Andrew paled, and his eyes grew wide. "Robin didn't
know?"

"No one knew, except a few of her friends, the doctor, and me," I shouted at him.

He shouted back. "And me. You wouldn't have figured it out without me."

"I didn't think you'd go blabbing like that." I was almost screaming.

He yelled back. "Everyone would have found out soon. She couldn't even see my math questions, that's why I read them aloud. It's not the end of the world."

"It's the end of her world."

"What?"

"Her family will make her give up her house. They'll make her move to an old folk's place, and that will . . ."

"Will what?"

I didn't want to think about the answer to that question. I sighed and lowered my voice. "Never mind, there's nothing we can do about it now. Please don't have a seizure because I was mad at you."

He looked indignant. "Now you're being stupid. No one causes my seizures, they just happen. Like farts."

Upset as I was, I had to smile. "Or hiccups?"

"Yup. How about I phone Robin and tell him I lied?"

"No use. He figured it out, I saw it on his face. He knows it's true."

"Then how about you let go of my shoulders before your fingers bore into my skin? You're hurting me."

I let go of him. "Sorry."

"What's going on down there?" Mom called from upstairs.

"Nothing," Andrew and I said together.

"Well, the 'nothing' is too noisy. Stop it. Go do your homework. Both of you."

"What's she doing home?"

I shrugged. "I guess the emergency at work solved itself. Or else she's working from her own computer, here."

"Keep it down. I've got a database to finish in half an hour."

"Okay, Mom," Andrew and I said in unison again and reached for our backpacks and our homework. He grabbed his and bounded up the stairs. I reached for mine, but it wasn't there. It was still in Robin's car.

The doorbell rang. When I opened the door, I wasn't surprised to see Robin, my backpack in his hand. Robin was pale and there was not a trace of a smile on his face.

"I've got to talk to you, Darrah."

"Who is it?" Mom called from upstairs. Without waiting for an answer, she started down the stairs, stopping when she saw Robin. "Oh, it's you," she said. "Thank you for driving Andrew and Darrah home, but aren't they early? I thought I'd have the house to myself for an hour longer."

"Mom!" I felt like shouting "Manners!" at her, the way she did at me so often.

"I'd like to talk to Darrah, please, Mrs. Patrick."

Mom was distracted. I could almost hear that database calling to her from her computer. "Okay," she said, turned around and went back upstairs.

I started for the kitchen, but Robin pulled me into the living room. "Let's talk in here," he said.

The living room? This was like the old days when a young man came to visit his girl and they had to sit in a formal parlour that was used only when the minister visited or after a funeral. Or when a young couple were "courting."

"Um, I can make tea or get us some pop or juice. Let's go to the kitchen."

"No, no distractions. In here."

He half-pushed me into the living room, sat me down on the sofa, then pulled up a chair and sat facing me.

"How long have you known?"

I wasn't stupid enough to ask "known what"—to play games.

"Not long."

"What's wrong with her eyes? And why did she tell you and not me?"

"She didn't tell me." I explained how I found the glasses and magnifiers, and began to wonder why she'd lied. "I knew there was something wrong once I found those," I said. "I should have figured it out earlier." I told him how she wanted me to read the newspapers and recipes aloud to her, and how Andrew and I had googled eye problems to narrow down the medical options.

"That's why her front stairs are such weird colours—the dark edges allow her to see where each step ends so she won't fall."

He nodded. "I wondered at her choosing that colour

scheme when she had me paint them. She used to wear her glasses all the time, and then for a while she had this big magnifying contraption that hung around her neck, sort of balanced on her chest, so that she could look through it when she read. I thought her eyes were getting better when she stopped wearing her glasses."

"She said glasses don't help anymore."

"What's macular degeneration? Is it curable?"

"Um . . . I don't know that much about it." I wasn't lying, I didn't know much, just what I'd read on a few medical sites.

"She's going blind, isn't she?"

"I don't know for sure."

He was silent for a long time, then "I have to tell Dad."

"No, don't! They don't have to know. I'll help her and you can do the garden and other things for her and Karen is there every morning and . . ."

He shook his head. "How old do you think she is?"

I hadn't really thought about it. "Seventy?" I guessed. Old was old.

He shook his head. "Not even close."

"Well how old is she?"

"We don't actually know. She won't tell anyone when she was born, but my dad thinks she's nearly ninety."

"Really?"

"Gran doesn't seem that old, does she?"

"Not usually," I said, honestly, omitting that lately I'd thought she looked old.

"But if she's losing her sight, she can't live alone, Darrah."

"She can, I told you—"

"Dad and Uncle Brad won't let her. They already worry about her being by herself in that house. No security, not even a decent lock on the door. Not that she ever locks it."

"But she's lived there for—"

"I know. I used to go there a lot when I was little. There was this awesome tree house and she always made gingerbread. Sometimes I got to sleep over, and she'd read me stories from these old books. Giants and fairies and magic spells. But my parents won't let her stay there once they know."

"So don't tell them."

"You don't understand. I fought—pleaded—for her when she broke her leg. My parents and uncle wanted to put her in a care home right then, to make sure she'd be safe with that cast on. They wanted to move her out of her house right away. I persuaded them not to do it, said I'd help her, do her driving, shopping. She promised she'd have Karen come every day, and would call us if she needed anything. A few weeks later, she told us about your school program and said you'd be there to help, too, so they let her stay. But they're still talking about how it's time for her to give up the house."

"So don't tell," I said again.

"What if something happens to her because of her eyesight? What if she falls again, or takes the wrong medicines because she can't read the labels on the bottles? If something awful happens, and I knew about her bad eyesight but hadn't told anyone, how do you think I'd feel?"

I was silent. I knew how Robin would feel if he didn't tell his father, and then Mrs. J. had an accident. I knew how horrible it felt to be responsible for something bad happening to someone else.

Dad came in, not surprised to see Robin. "Hi, it's Robin, right? I recognized your car from when you picked Darrah up the other day. Hey, Darrah, got any ideas for dinner? It's late."

It was—almost seven and dark. Even if Mom was too busy to want to eat, Andrew would be hungry. "Maybe mac and cheese. I'll put cottage cheese in it to make it creamier. Maybe some sliced hot dogs, too, if there are any. I hadn't planned on cooking tonight, sorry Dad."

"Andrew okay?"

"What?"

"He hasn't had another . . ." he swallowed hard and then said it. He said the "S" word. "He hasn't had another seizure?"

"No, Dad, he's fine."

Robin stood up. "Got to go," he said abruptly and walked out.

"That young man looks troubled," said my father.

"He had a shock today."

I saw the question beginning to form on Dad's lips, and stood up myself. "Let's see what we can find for dinner, okay? Why don't you check on Mom, see if she had anything planned. If not, mac 'n cheese it is. Or we can order in."

◆ ◆ ◆

Of course, Robin did tell his parents. The second I walked into Mrs. J.'s house, I knew. She sat on the tall stool by the kitchen counter and glowered at me. "Why did you talk to your brother about my eyesight? You promised not to let anyone know."

"I didn't tell him, he helped me figure it out using his computer because I wasn't allowed to use mine except for school work. I'm sorry."

"Not as sorry as I am. Both my sons were here this morning, didn't even go to their jobs. Fistfuls of brochures from those places: Sunny Side Residence; Retirement Haven; Silver Strands Home; The Imperial—" She waved them in front of me. They had pictures of smiling old people puttering about in gardens, or playing cards, or having tea with other smiling old people.

"My sons read the brochures to me, loudly. As if something was wrong with my ears, not with my eyes. As if I were going deaf, not blind."

She shoved the pile of shiny brochures off the counter. I started to pick them up, but she shook her head. "Let the damned things lie there. I want them out of my sight."

I started picking them up anyway, wanting to get them off the floor so she wouldn't slip on them. She didn't notice.

"My sons told me to choose a place I wanted to go, or they'd decide for me. Damn it, I gave them that power of attorney years ago, never figured they'd use it against me like this."

"I don't know what that is. Power of . . . ?"

"It's a legal document I signed, so that if I'm brain dead or really sick or just plain ditzy, they can handle my money and take care of me."

"They are trying to take care of you."

She glared at me. "Whose side are you on, girl? They want to warehouse me! Bet their wives are already arguing over which real estate agent should handle the sale of my house."

"Andrew didn't know that it was a secret. He felt terrible."

"It's not the kid's fault. I knew they'd find out soon. Grab me the tea strainer."

"What kind of tea shall I make?"

"Don't want tea, just the strainer." She held it in her hands for a few moments, running her fingers over the long handle before she replaced it in the silver dish that kept the wet tea leaves from dripping onto the tablecloth.

Then she thrust it at me. "Here. Take it."

"What?"

"Take it. Keep it. It was a wedding present, sterling silver, from my grandmother, the one who painted the china. I want you to have it, now that you've learned how to make a decent pot of tea."

"I can't . . ."

"Damn it, girl, I can still make my own decisions about my own things. Take it."

I didn't understand why it was so important to her, but I

took the silver strainer and its small silver dish. The handle of the strainer was decorated with starfish and sea shells, so worn in spots that it was hard to see what some of the engravings were.

"Thank you." I didn't know what else to say. Now was not a good time for questions, that was obvious. "Thank you very much." What was I going to do with a silver tea strainer?

"Put that in your backpack and take out some paper."

"Paper?"

"Don't you use paper in school anymore? Something to write on, five or six pages. And a pen. But first, grab me two of those pills in the cupboard up where I keep the tea. And a glass of water. Then sit down, I've got a job for you, and it has to be done today."

Chapter Fourteen

I TUCKED THE SILVER tea strainer and its dish into my lunch bag, grabbed a half dozen pieces of loose leaf-paper from my binder and went back to the kitchen.

"Pull up that other stool and sit beside me," Mrs. J. commanded. "I can't see what you're writing, but at least I can see that you're writing something."

I brought the stool over and climbed up onto it. "I'm ready. How do you want the page set up?"

"Use note form, no need for full sentences, but make sure your writing is legible. I'll help with spelling."

"Both my handwriting and spelling are good," I protested.

"We'll see. Begin, 'The Queen Anne chair—'"

"The what?"

"Queen Anne (that's Anne with an 'e') chair is for Karen, she's always liked it. My sterling silver flatware is for . . ."

I wrote for half an hour. The dining room table and chairs, her jewellery (not much, an engagement ring, a wedding ring and a string of real pearls), her good dinner china, crystal glasses, the big armchair—every item I wrote down was followed by someone's name. Once in a while she'd stop and ask me to go back and make a change. "No, cross her out; I know where that will be better appreciated."

My fingers were cramping. Her directions would have been so much easier to key into a laptop, instead of writing out by hand. "Can we stop for a bit? My hand hurts."

"Yes, let's take a break. Put the kettle on. Regular tea, we'll have to use the tea bags. Don't know where I put my tea strainer."

The look on my face must have shown my shock, because she laughed, and put a hand on my arm. "It's all right, I'm not going senile. I know exactly where my strainer is, I gave it to you. That was my rather sorry attempt at a joke."

"It wasn't funny!"

"I apologize. Now get that tea going."

When we were settled again, mugs of tea in front of us, she returned to her itemizing.

"The sterling tea strainer—write your own name after that, girl, just to make sure everyone knows I gave it to you and you didn't steal it. You don't want to have to go through another one of those circle things, do you?"

I shuddered. "No, thanks. One circle was enough."

"Next item: Grandma's painted tea set, six each of cups, saucers, side plates, and two matching serving plates are for Robin."

"Robin? Really? He'll be thrilled."

She grinned. "Won't he? I hope he doesn't let his mother use it; she's one of the clumsiest women I've ever known. Oh, and make a note that he already owns my car and no one is to try to take it away from him."

I took a sip of tea; it was too hot and burned my mouth. "Ouch," I said. My eyes blurred, and I fought back tears.

"What's wrong?"

"I burned my mouth ... you're giving everything away because they're going to make you move. To one of those warehouses that you hate."

"Don't worry about it."

"It's my fault that your family found out about your eyes. If I hadn't made you fall and break your leg—"

"It's no one's fault, girl. It's life." A surprisingly strong hand gripped my arm. "You are not to blame yourself, understand? Promise me you won't blame yourself, no matter what happens."

"But if I hadn't pulled that alarm, then ..."

"Then my family would have found out anyway; my eyesight is rapidly getting worse. I couldn't hide it much longer. Besides, I enjoy having you here. You're going to be a good cook."

I sniffled, still fighting tears.

"Stop whimpering. Grab a tissue and blow your nose. We've still got a few things to add to that list."

A few minutes later she announced, "That's it, we're done." I shook out the cramp in my hand again, and the doorbell rang.

I went to answer it and ushered in Mr. Allen. He chose the purple slippers today.

"You're right on time, David. Let's get to it."

"I'm ready, Janie. We've got an hour until my office closes, we'll be there in plenty of time. I told them to wait for us, even if we were a bit late."

"Office?" I was completely confused.

Mr. Allen smiled at me. "I still practise a bit of law, once in a while, although I seldom go to my office, even though my name is still on the door. I started that law firm forty years ago."

"A lawyer?" I couldn't help it, my eyes slid to his purple clad feet. "Really?"

"Indeed. And although I am retired, I can still help an old friend with a codicil or two."

"What's a codicil?"

"What you just wrote down," said Mrs. J. "Instructions that go with a will, so that relatives don't fight over who gets what."

"We'll have what Darrah wrote for you notarized at my office," said Mr. Allen. "Then it's legal. Did you decide who will get your grandmother's china, Janie?"

"Robin, of course," she said.

"Oh, I'm sure he'll be delighted," said Mr. Allen, chuckling. "Shall we get started?"

"If you'll help me up, David, we'll work at the dining room table." He put his briefcase on the floor, and gallantly offered her one arm, the one not holding his cane. She groaned as she stood up, then swayed, grabbing at his arm for support. I jumped up to help, but she scowled and shook her head. "Been sitting too long; a bit dizzy. Don't fuss."

The two of them made their way arm-in-arm to the dining room, their canes moving almost in unison as they walked. Mr. Allen seated her at the table before pulling up a chair for himself. "Darrah," he called, "could you bring me my brief-case and those papers you were working on, please? Then pull the sliding doors closed when you leave the room."

"But . . . but what will I do?"

"Oh, do anything you like, girl. We won't be long."

They weren't. I had just organized my math homework when I heard the sliding door open, and they emerged, Mrs. J. again clinging to Mr. Allen's arm. "Could you get my brief-case?" he asked. It was on the dining room table, closed tightly and there was no sign of my loose-leaf paper with the notes.

"We'll drop you off at home," said Mrs. J. "Get your stuff together."

"But I'm supposed to stay until six."

"I'll give you credit for your whole time. Let's go."

I went.

◆ ◆ ◆

Two days later when I climbed the orange stairs, everything seemed back to normal. Mrs. J. sat on her tall stool, a mug of tea in front of her. She didn't look as tired as she had on Monday, and she smiled as I came in.

"It's December," she announced.

"Has been for a while."

"Time to make Yule Log. It's our family version of the traditional Christmas cake."

"But . . ." I stopped, not knowing how to ask the question that had been worrying me since I last saw her.

"But what?"

"Don't you have to move? I mean—"

"You mean why am I still here? Not off playing bridge at Silver Strands Rest Home with other dithering relics?"

"Um . . . yes."

She grinned. "Told my sons I deserved one last Christmas in my own home. Lectured them up one side and down the other, asked how they could even think of making me move at Christmas time. Reminded them of all the Christmases they'd spent here, how when they were little they'd run down the hall in their pajamas, eager to see what Santa had brought. I dredged up every memory of Christmas in this house I could think of. Caught Robin's dad wiping at tears and trying not to let me see."

"You guilted them!"

"Indeed I did. Very thoroughly. There will be no more talk of me leaving my home until the new year."

I burst out laughing. "Must have been a great performance."

"One of my best," she said. "Academy award quality, if I do say so myself. So, grab the recipe box and look up 'Yule Log.' Today we'll make a shopping list; we need nuts and candied peel and other things I don't keep in the pantry. Karen will go shopping for me, and the next time you come you can make it."

I wrote out the list of ingredients. "Unsalted Brazil nuts, maraschino cherries, one jar red, one jar green . . ."

Mrs. J. had to explain what maraschino cherries were; I'd never seen one. "They come in jars, sort of like candied fruit, in a sweet syrup. They used to be popular in cocktails, back when everyone served cocktails—those fancy drinks with olives, cherries or tiny onions and different types of juices and syrups."

Once the shopping list was finished, I asked, "What else will I do today?"

"Help Robin. He's bringing a tree. I'm not decorating it all by myself. But first, grab that box of apple juice on the counter and let's get some Christmas cider simmering."

Apple juice, orange slices, spices—it didn't take long to mix the cider. I put the pot on the stove, on low, and put the spices away. I was just setting out mugs and cookies on a tray when the doorbell rang.

A huge tree filled the doorway. From somewhere deep in the branches, Robin's voice emerged. "Don't know if this is going to fit through the door. Gran said to get a big one, so I did."

Between the two of us, Robin and I maneuvered the tree into the front hall. Mrs. J. hovered and issued instructions. "Robin, grab a sheet from the linen cupboard, one of the old flannel ones. Darrah, help him wrap it around the tree, then the two of you might be able to get it into the living room without breaking half the branches."

"Okay, Gran, but you have to move out of the way so I can get past."

I hung onto the tree, while Robin wriggled around me, returning with a sheet. We managed to swaddle the tree, and get it into the living room. There was a red metal stand waiting for it, and we gently eased the tree in.

The top two inches of the tree bent against the ceiling, but otherwise it fit perfectly. Mrs. J. gave more instructions, "It's leaning, pull it more to your right, girl. Robin, make sure those screws are tight enough or it won't stay straight. Move it to the right, no, that's too much, a bit left. Hold it steady, now."

Robin stood on a chair and snipped off enough of the top so the tree reached the ceiling without bending, then all three of us stood back and admired it. "Perfect," announced Mrs. J. "Good choice, Robin. Now, go get the decorations, the box is on the top cupboard shelf in—"

"In the storage room in the basement. Yes, Gran, I've done this before." He left, followed slowly by Mrs. J. who shouted instructions from the top of the basement stairs.

I stood alone by the tree, smelling the forest. My family had always used an artificial tree, one with the lights already attached. For a while we'd used a silvery aluminum tree with red lights which had belonged to my grandma. I loved the way the lights sparkled in that tree, reflecting off the shiny needles. But when I was twelve, Dad decided we should have a tree that looked more like a tree, so we got a new one. Every year he hauled it up from the basement and set it up proudly. "Can hardly tell it from the real thing, can you?" he'd ask and we'd all nod and agree with him.

But our tree was nothing like a real one. I breathed in this tree, and touched a branch. The needles pricked at my wrist; the branch was rough and felt cool. It looked and smelled like Christmas should.

Chapter Fifteen

ROBIN CAME BACK, face flushed, a large box balanced in his arms. Mrs. J. issued more instructions. "Set it on the coffee table. Careful, those ornaments are breakable."

"Yes, Gran." Robin sighed as he lowered the box. "I did this last year, and the year before, I know all about your precious glass ornaments." He had a strand of cobweb stuck to his head, dangling over one ear like a lace scarf, and a dusty smudge on his forehead.

Both Mrs. J. and I laughed. "Go wash," she said to him. "Then we'll get started."

The box was packed to the brim. I opened it and began removing boxes of glass ornaments, some the usual round shape, but some that looked like teardrops. The small boxes they were packed in were so old the cardboard had yellowed, and the narrow strips of cardboard separating the ornaments were bent and torn.

"Lights first," commanded Mrs. J. as Robin pulled out a string of old fashioned lights, large ones, not the tiny mini-lights. We all cheered when he plugged in the string and every single bulb lit up.

"That's good, Gran. I don't know if you can buy replacement bulbs that size anymore."

Robin and I stood on either side of the tree, passing the lights back and forth as we wound them around the tree, ending with a yellow light at the very top.

Mrs. J. had been pulling ornaments from the box. "Here," she announced. "This one goes on first. I'll hang it, then the two of you can do the rest of the decorations."

She leaned on her cane as she reached up the tree, her hand trembling as she tried to hook a loop of string over a branch. I went to help, but Robin shook his head. "Gran has to do it. It's tradition."

The ornament finally secured, Mrs. J. moved to the couch. She sat down, both hands clasped over the cane in front of her. "What are you waiting for? Get busy."

I chose a golden teardrop ornament and deliberately hung it near where Mrs. J. had put her decoration. I saw it wasn't much, a lopsided star, probably cardboard, covered in what looked like tinfoil with a loop of yarn glued to the back. The branches moved as I hung my ornament, and the motion made the star twist. It was definitely covered in tinfoil, I could see a strip of yellowing tape at the back, holding the foil together. What's so special about this? I wondered.

As if she had read my thoughts, Mrs. J. explained. "It's from the first tree my husband and I had as newlyweds. It was a small tree, not much bigger than a table lamp. We put it in a big ugly flower vase someone had given us for a wedding present and used rocks to hold it steady. We couldn't afford to buy lights or ornaments, so we made decorations ourselves. Popcorn strings, ribbon bows and ten silver stars. This is the only one left now. It's been on every Christmas tree I've ever had."

"It's lovely," I lied.

"No, it's not. Don't be silly. But it's part of my life, and I like to see it on the tree."

It didn't take us long to empty the box. I left Robin carefully hanging icicles, one flimsy strand at a time, and went to get the cider and cookies.

"Bring two of my pills, when you come back. And a glass of water."

I did, and once she'd gulped the pills, and Robin and I each had a mug of cider and a couple of cookies in front of us, she asked him to turn off the overhead lights.

We sat in darkness except for the lights of the Christmas tree, sipping cider. No one spoke for a while, and finally I heard Mrs. J. sigh.

"Thank you both. I'll always remember this tree."

"No problem, Gran. Glad to help. I'll do it next . . . I mean, I like setting up your tree . . ."

"It's all right, Robin. We'll enjoy this one, and not worry about next year."

"I wish you didn't have to move."

"I do, too, but it has to be. We all know that, don't we?"

He nodded, started to say something, then his voice faltered and he stopped.

"Time for you both to go. Take the tray into the kitchen, girl, then leave it. David's coming over later, he'll help wash up the mugs. But first clean up this mess."

I started putting the tissue paper and fragile empty boxes away. When I was finished, Robin picked up the box. "I'll take it downstairs." I heard him in the kitchen, blowing his nose. "Dust in my eyes," he said loud enough for us to hear, but I knew he was wiping away tears.

"Goodbye, Mrs. J. See you Monday."

She nodded goodbye from her seat on the couch, her eyes still on the Christmas tree. "Good. We'll make the Yule Log. Double recipe so you can take one home for your family."

"Thanks," I said. It had started snowing while we were decorating the tree. A layer of flakes dusted the ground, and snow had settled on the car windshield. Robin brushed it off before climbing in. He started the engine and turned on the wipers to clear the last of the snow. The car filled with an awkward silence. This was the first time I'd been alone with him since the day Andrew had told him about his grand-mother's eyes. It hadn't been too bad while we were putting the tree up, but now I didn't know what to say.

I swallowed. "I'm sorry that Andrew—"

He cut me off. "It's okay, really. All the clues were there, someone in the family would have figured it out soon."

"I'm so sorry," I said again.

"It will be all right," he said, as much to himself as to me. "After Christmas the whole family—everyone, my brothers, cousins, a few wives, even kids—will be in town. Gran won't let anyone stay with her, but we'll all help her pack up and get rid of her stuff. Then we'll move her. It will be all right."

More silence. I was thinking, no, it won't be all right for Mrs. J., not at all right. She'd enjoyed watching her Christmas tree being decorated, making sure that Robin and I did it the way she wanted. When she'd hung the homemade silver star, her face had softened and she'd smiled. I hoped someone would pack that star for her to take to her new place. I hoped that Robin and I could decorate a tree for her next year.

"I can go and see her in the . . . in her new place every day after school," said Robin. "At least, until I go away to university."

"I'll go see her, too. I should be getting my driver's license soon." Once the sanctions were done, I could apply for my learner's, Mom and Dad had promised. "I'll go see her, especially when you're away."

I might be able to get that learner's license sooner than I had thought I could, thanks to Andrew. The doctor had put him on another new medication. He said he felt better, and so far he hadn't had a seizure. Last night he talked about going back to soccer. Mom said she was too busy to drive him to practices, even if the doctor said it was all right for him to play, which she doubted. I'd offered to take him and watch him. "It would be much easier if I had my driver's license," I'd said, hopefully. Mom and Dad had exchanged glances.

"Maybe," said my father.

"We'll talk about it," said my mother.

"I'm making spaghetti for dinner," I said to Robin. "Want to stay?"

"Grandma's recipe?"

"Of course. But I leave out the garlic. My family doesn't like garlic—yet."

"Too bad. Don't know if I can eat spaghetti without garlic in the sauce. But I'm willing to try."

"Good, you can chop the onions. They make me cry."

He parked in front of our house. The lights were on, it looked welcoming. We hadn't put up our Christmas tree yet, but Dad said we'd do it on the weekend.

Andrew was deep in a *Star Trek* rerun. When he saw Robin, he looked uncomfortable. "Uh . . . hi," he said.

"Hey, Andrew," said Robin cheerfully, as if nothing had happened. "I'm invited to dinner. Tell me the truth, how's Darrah's spaghetti sauce? Any good?"

"Better than the stuff from the pizza place," said Andrew. "You want to watch *Voyager* with me?"

"Sure." Robin plopped down beside him.

"He can't. He promised to help me in the kitchen. Besides, you've seen this episode hundreds of times. Even I've seen it twice. Haven't you got homework?"

Andrew flicked off the TV, muttering, "You're getting worse than Mom. She didn't even notice that I'm still watching TV."

He climbed the stairs, still grumbling. Mom's voice floated down. "Is Darrah home yet? It's her night to cook dinner."

"Just going to start it, Mom," I shouted up the stairs. "Ready in half an hour."

She didn't answer, I guess she'd gone back to her work, dealing with whatever office crisis had happened today.

Robin didn't take long peeling and chopping the onion, then he pulled up a chair and watched me. I browned the hamburger, tossed the chopped onion and a grated carrot into the pan. Then, when the onion turned golden, I dumped in the can of tomato sauce. I was digging in the cupboard wondering where I'd put the oregano, when he asked, "Did you talk to your parents?"

"About what?"

"About going out with me."

I turned around so suddenly that I nearly bumped my head on the cupboard door. "You still want me to? After . . ."

"Yes. It isn't your fault my grandmother is going blind."

"But it is my fault she broke her leg," I blurted out, then immediately, desperately, wished I hadn't.

"I know."

"You know?" I wanted to run out of the kitchen, not look

at him, not talk about the fire alarm, the circle, the whole embarrassing episode. "How?"

"Gran told me, back when you first came to help her. She didn't want to, but I kept badgering her about this school 'work program' she said you were doing. I know there's no program like that, so I made her tell me the truth."

I sat down, shaken. Robin went to the stove and took over stirring the sauce. He turned the heat down, then came and stood in front of me, his hands on my shoulders.

"It's okay, Darrah. No one else knows. Gran told me it wasn't all your fault, that if she'd been holding onto the railing she wouldn't have fallen. She said it was her own stupidity, thinking she could handle the stairs."

"But . . ."

"She didn't want to do that circle thing, but the constable told her that if she didn't you'd end up in court, and that would be serious trouble for you."

"But . . ."

"Once she met you at the circle, she liked you."

"But . . ."

"But what?"

"If you've known all along, why—"

"Why don't I hate you?"

"Um . . . yes."

"Because everyone makes mistakes. Because you care about my grandma. Because it's been good for her to have you there. She loves teaching you how to cook."

"But . . ."

"And because I like you."

He moved his hands to either side of my face; the onion smell on them made tears prickle behind my eyelids. He tilted my face up and looked at me, smiling.

"I really like you, Darrah," he said and kissed me.

Chapter Sixteen

ROBIN CAME OVER on Saturday and helped my family put up our Christmas tree. Then he held the ladder while Dad draped lights on the bare branches of the flowering cherry tree in the front yard, and shovelled the new snow off the walkway. He was back again on Sunday. He helped Andrew with his math homework and stayed for dinner again—take-out pizza this time. Mom was cooking.

"That young man's been here all weekend," my Dad complained to me as he was loading the dishwasher. "Don't you two ever go out?"

"We'd love to," said Robin. "Would it be all right if Darrah and I went to a movie tonight?"

"Didn't know you were right behind me. Sorry," said Dad. "But, sure, go ahead." And there went Consequence Number Three, zapped away by the Christmas spirit. Mom didn't seem to notice when we said goodbye, but she called to me before we were out the front door. "Darrah, wait a minute."

As the novels say, my heart "sank." Right into my boots. She'd remembered that I was grounded. But all she said was, "It's a school night, come home right after the movie's over."

"Thanks, Mom," I said. "Thanks a lot!"

"We won't be late," promised Robin. As he turned to open the door, Mom winked at me. "Have fun," she said.

"Thanks," was all I managed to mumble. I was too surprised to say anything else. Mom hadn't forgotten the consequence; she had deliberately set me free. Oh, I love the Christmas spirit!

"Thought you said you were grounded," Robin said.

"I thought so, too."

"Must be my charm that changed their minds."

"Charm? Is that what that was? I didn't notice."

I don't remember much about the movie. What I remember is my fingers, sticky with the pop I'd spilled, sticking to Robin's when he held my hand. I remember kissing him, both of us with buttery, salty lips, tasting of popcorn. Neither of us noticed when the credits began to roll and the house lights came up.

Someone trying to get past our seats said, "Break it up, you two, and let me get out of here," and we jumped apart.

I sat in the car outside my house, looked at the glow from

the Christmas tree through the windows and the lights on the cherry tree in the front yard, and thought that life was pretty sweet.

"School night," Robin reminded me.

"I know, I'm going."

He leaned across the seat and gave me a peck on the cheek. "Now, get out of here. I'll see you at Gran's tomorrow." I stood on the sidewalk, waved as he drove off and felt a silly grin spread across my face.

I read somewhere that you should never tempt the fates by letting them know when you are happy. I should have remembered that because, as I walked in the front door, I could hear Mom's voice, shouting at Dad to call 911. My boots still on my feet, dripping clumps of snow, I flew up the stairs. Mom and Dad crouched beside Andrew who was in his pajamas, flat on the floor outside the bathroom door. This was a strong seizure: his eyelids flicked up and down so quickly they were a blur, his head rolled from side to side, his arms and legs jerked. I pulled off my jacket, wadded it up and crouched down to put it under Andrew's head.

"How long has it been going on?" I asked.

"I don't know, I forgot to count," said Dad.

"Okay, I'll begin counting from a minute and we'll estimate later." I started counting off the seconds, "Sixty-one, sixty-two, sixty-three . . ." I had reached one hundred and ten when Andrew grew still. His eyelids shut, his legs stopped jerking. It was over.

"Oh, Andrew, oh . . ." Mom burst into tears. Dad stood up

and went to her and put his hands on her shoulders. "It's okay, it will be okay."

"Again?" complained a weak voice. "Not again, please." Andrew was awake.

"Just a short one, not too bad," I lied. "How are you feeling?"

"Tired. I want to go to back to bed."

We helped him stand, and while Mom and Dad tucked him into bed, I went downstairs and took off my boots and hung up my coat. There were slushy footprints all over the front hall; I grabbed some paper towel and wiped them up, and followed the prints up the stairs, blotting at the melting snow. Then I went to the kitchen and put the kettle on. This family needed a good hot cup of tea. Tomorrow, I'd get Dad to buy half a dozen clocks, put them all over the house, so no matter where Andrew had a seizure, we could tell how long it lasted. With strong seizures, like the last two had been, we needed to be accurate about their length; after five minutes it was time to call for help. I pulled out the seizure diary that the doctor had asked Mom to keep, wrote down the date and time, 11 p.m., then put three minutes with a question mark. I'd counted just under two minutes, but I knew that neither Mom nor Dad would be able to estimate how long Andrew had been seizing before I arrived. No matter how short his seizure actually was, it always seemed to go on forever. The only way to know for sure how long it had been was to count seconds or keep your eye on a clock.

The kettle boiled. I poured water over two chamomile tea bags in the pre-warmed pot and waited for my parents to come downstairs.

♦ ♦ ♦

The next day Mrs. J. snapped at me the moment I walked into the kitchen. "You're late, girl. I've been waiting."

"I missed the first bus, sorry."

"Let's get started, we've got a lot to do today."

I found two bread pans and the baking paper, then cut the paper and lined the pans with it as she instructed. Paper? In the oven? I was doubtful, but Mrs. J. always knew what she was doing. "It's baking or parchment paper," she explained. "It won't burn and the cake won't stick to the pan. Wonderful stuff, been around for years."

Baking paper might have been around for years, but it was new to me. I measured flour, drained jars of maraschino cherries, chopped dates and roasted whole Brazil nuts. I was stirring the mixture, watched carefully by Mrs. J., when Robin arrived.

"Just in time," she said. "Everyone has to stir the Christmas cake. It means we'll all have good luck for the year. Pass him the bowl, girl."

I did, puzzled. Robin obediently pushed the wooden spoon through the dough, then gave the bowl to his grandmother. She motioned for him to put it on the counter, took a deep breath and slowly gave the batter a few turns. "Tradition is tradition. You remember that. Everyone in the house has to stir the batter."

"Sure," I said. "I'll write it down when I copy the recipe, if you'll let me borrow the recipe card."

"You're writing recipes down? My recipes?"

"Not all yours. I wrote my barbecued chicken soup from scratch."

She smiled at me, her earlier bad temper forgotten. "Good. Keep doing that. Don't forget to make notes if you change proportions or alter the recipe and it turns out well. Or terribly. Otherwise you'll forget what you did."

I nodded, and took over stirring the cake. It was thick and lumpy; there didn't seem to be enough flour in it to hold the ingredients together while they baked. I managed to get most of it into the pans without making a mess, and used a spatula to finish emptying the bowl. I shook the pans to level the dough, popped them into the oven, set the oven timer, then began washing up the cooking utensils. No dishwasher in this house. Except me, and probably Karen when she came over.

Robin picked up a drying towel. "I'll help."

Maybe there was something about the way he looked at me, or maybe I blushed, because Mrs. J. laughed. "Thought you two would be a good match. Had that first date yet?"

I could feel the blush growing hotter across my face. "Um . . ."

"Gran, that's none of your business."

"Uh-huh, thought so."

"Mrs. J., I don't think . . ." Then I stopped. In a way it *was* her business. "Yes," I admitted. "He is kinda nice, once you get used to him."

"Well, this calls for a celebration. I'll have two pills and a fresh cup of tea. Unfortunately the Yule Log won't be ready for a while, so we'll have to make do with the shortbread Karen brought."

We had tea and shortbread in the living room. Mrs. J. didn't eat anything, but sipped slowly at her tea. "I think this is the best Christmas tree I've ever had," she said. "Except, maybe, for my first one."

I had a vision of that scrawny tree, hardly more than a branch, balanced carefully in a vase, decorated only with red ribbon bows and homemade silver stars.

"Do you have a picture of that tree?"

"Now, why would you want to see a silly thing like that, girl? But no, I don't. We had a camera, but no money to buy film or get the pictures developed."

"That's too bad. It would be a good picture to show at Christmas time."

"I've many good memories; don't need pictures to remind me of them," she said, then sighed.

"Get out of here, you two. Karen's coming over in an hour. She'll take the baking out of the oven."

"Still working on those exercises with Karen, Gran?"

"Not today. Today she's helping me with Christmas cards."

"They'll be late," said Robin. "Christmas is only ten days away."

Reluctantly, I picked up the tray and carried it into the kitchen. After a few minutes Mrs. J. followed, leaning on her walker, pushing it ahead of her.

"Why are you . . ." I began, shocked to see her using it.

Robin was behind her, and he shook his head furiously. He didn't want me to mention the walker.

Mrs. J. saw me staring at the walker and frowned. She didn't want me to mention it either.

"Go help my grandson find a Christmas gift for his mother. He always gets her something practical and she hates it."

"I thought the juicer was a good idea," he said indignantly. "Why didn't you tell me she didn't like kitchen stuff, Gran?"

"I've told you now, haven't I?"

He hugged her. "Thanks. You're sure Darrah won't get into trouble for leaving early?"

"No, she's earned her hours today. Now get going."

I tossed the orange slippers into the basket, and Robin and I left.

"She's up to something," he said as we climbed into the car.

"She's using the walker," I said at the same time. "She said she never would."

"Gran says she's fighting a cold and it's made her weak. She doesn't use the walker all the time. Keeps it parked in the living room, out of sight." He glanced at his watch. "So, we've got an hour. The mall?"

The mall? I hadn't been there since September. I wondered if I'd recognize the place.

"Let me call home and check," I said, wondering if my ungrounding extended to going to the mall. The home phone went right to voicemail; someone was using it. "Mrs. J. asked me to go with Robin to pick out a gift for his mother. I hope that's okay, I'll be home right after six. I'm not cooking tonight so . . ." Robin took the phone from my hand.

"Thanks a lot, Mrs. Patrick, I really need help. Grandma sent Darrah away early, she's not skipping out." He hung up.

"Let's go shopping!"

All I could do was grin at him. "Let's."

Chapter Seventeen

ON WEDNESDAY, MRS. J. called to me as soon as I walked in her door. "In the living room, girl."

The lights sparkled on the Christmas tree. She was sitting on the couch, staring at them, her walker within reach. "Just having a sit-down before we start work," she explained.

"Shall I make you some tea?"

"No. Yes. Go into the kitchen and start the kettle. I'll be right there."

She wasn't "right" there. I heard a muffled groan as she pulled herself up from the couch, then the soft swish of the walker's rubber wheels as she navigated her way into the kitchen. "This thing's kinda handy, once you get used to it," she said. From the carrier basket she pulled out an empty glass, a mug and two plates and put them on the counter. "Had my lunch by the Christmas tree."

Handy? "That damned thing" was what she'd called it when she first saw it. The kettle was boiling, so I poured water in the teapot to pre-warm it, then carried her dishes to the sink.

"Are you feeling okay, Mrs. J?"

"A bit tired, that's all. Probably the thought of all the work ahead of me."

"Work?"

"The family's already started arriving. Right after Christmas they'll all be over here, cluttering up the place, figuring out who gets what piece of furniture, packing away my china and digging around in the basement, looking for treasures."

"Oh."

"Go ahead, ask. You want to."

"Have they found you a . . . a new home?"

"I chose one myself, put down the deposit. Move-in day is January fifteenth."

"I'm sorry."

"Told you, it's not your fault. It's life. How's that tea coming?"

We made church window cookies: melted chocolate, nuts and tiny coloured marshmallows. "I've never had these cookies before," I said.

"They're actually more a candy than a cookie, but I used to

make them for the boys. And the grandkids. They'll all be here this Christmas. Thought they'd like them."

"I'll come to your new place and help you cook, Mrs. J. We can make them next year, too."

"Not much of a kitchen where I'm going. Microwave, small fridge. Eat most of my meals in the dining room with the other old farts."

"Maybe they'll be nice old fa . . . people and you'll like them."

"Maybe."

I didn't know what to say next, so I focused on rolling up "logs" of cookie mixture in plastic wrap. The logs would go into the fridge and the cookies would be sliced off as needed. No baking. This was the easiest recipe I'd made in this kitchen. I scraped around the bowl, then licked the spoon. One of the best tasting recipes, too. Andrew would like this; I'd copy down the recipe before I left and add it to my collection.

It was barely five when Robin arrived. He helped me wash up, sampled a not-quite-firm (it hadn't been in the fridge long enough to chill properly) church window cookie, then looked at his grandmother expectantly.

"Go ahead, have fun," she said. "Don't have anything else for the girl to do, might as well get the two of you out of my hair."

"But . . ."

"No sense you sitting around here, girl. Take a roll of cookies and one of those Yule Logs you made."

"I don't want to leave so early again," I protested.

Robin looked offended. "What? You'd prefer Gran's company to mine?"

"No, it's just that . . ."

"It's all right. Go ahead, enjoy yourself. I don't need you anymore."

"But . . ."

"We're leaving, Gran."

"Okay, I'll see you Monday, Mrs. J."

"No, not until after Christmas. I've got lots of help right now; the house is going to be full of visitors wanting to look after me. Take some time off; you've earned it."

"Until after Christmas? Are you sure?"

"What's wrong with your ears? Go, scoot, skedaddle, leave."

I took a foil-wrapped Yule Log and a roll of church window cookies out of the fridge.

"I hope you have a good Christmas, Mrs. J."

"You too. Come over here for a moment. There's something for you in the basket of that walker."

"But I didn't get you a present or even a card!"

"No need to. They'll just get thrown out when I move."

I picked up a thin package wrapped in shiny blue paper, no name on it. "This?"

"Yes. Mind you don't open it until Christmas day. Promise?"

"I won't. Thank you."

She held out her hand. It took me a minute, but then I realized what she wanted me to do. I tucked the blue package, the cookies and the cake under my left arm, and reached out my right hand. Mrs. J. took it, but instead of shaking it, she held it for a few seconds, then put her other hand on top of it. "Have a good Christmas, Darrah."

◆ ◆ ◆

Robin and I spent a lot of time together the week before Christmas. We discovered Fong's Chinese Market, just a street up from the big underground mall. That little store was packed full of things I'd never seen before: jars of pickled fishy stuff, all sorts of noodles, rice crackers of all shapes and sizes, shelves of sauces and spices and boxes of vegetables all piled together in such a small space you could hardly move. The owner, I guess she was Mrs. Fong, was very helpful when I told her I wanted to cook some Chinese dishes. She sold me a clump of something called baby bok choy. It had thick white stems on the bottom and a leafy green top, with one tiny yellow flower in the green part—it looked like a thicker-stemmed clump of celery topped with romaine lettuce. I also bought a bag of fortune cookies, a big bottle of soy sauce and a jar of something called hoisin sauce. Mrs. Fong explained how to use it. "First cook chicken in oven half hour, then put sauce on, cook another half hour, very good."

"I've had it in restaurants," said Robin. "I love hoisin chicken."

Mrs. Fong nodded. "You also make fried rice, easy like pie. You fix stir-fry vegetables, too: carrots, bok choy, mushroom, broccoli, peppers, soy sauce. You come back another day and I tell you more Chinese food."

The internet had lots of Chinese recipes; it was easy to find one for every dish she mentioned. I found recipes that didn't look too complicated, nothing that called for making a sauce from scratch or using something I had never tasted, and wrote them down on cards for my recipe collection.

On Christmas Eve, I cooked Chinese food and it was better than any takeout we'd ever had. I bought a package of won tons in the frozen food section of the grocery store, made a chicken stock, added seasonings and the won tons. We started with soup, then we had stir-fried vegetables, hoisin chicken, fried rice and finished with ice cream and fortune cookies for dessert.

There wasn't a bit of anything (except some ice cream and six fortune cookies) left over when the meal was over. Robin had joined us for dinner. He and Dad pushed back their chairs at almost the same moment.

"Excellent, Darrah," said my father. "Well done."

"Not bad," said Robin. "Although, a few more mushrooms in the stir fry would have improved it." I threw a fortune cookie at him.

"Food fight!" announced Andrew gleefully, grabbing for another fortune cookie.

"Not in my dining room," said Mom. "Why don't you go outside and have a snowball fight instead? Maybe shovel the walk, while you're out there. I'll clean up."

"I'm coming, too," said Dad.

"Nice try," Mom said, "but you're on kitchen duty with me."

It had started snowing in the morning, and snow had kept coming down all day. There was a lot of the white stuff by now, clean and fluffy. Perfect for packing into snowballs.

When we came back inside, one lopsided snowman, three snow angels and a lot of snowballs later, the kitchen was spotless. Mom and Dad sat on the couch in the living room, Mom's head on Dad's shoulder, mugs of eggnog on the coffee table in front of them.

"Oh, yuck!" said Andrew. "Do you *have* to?"

Mom smiled at him. "It's Christmas. Come over here and we'll give you a snuggle, too."

Andrew fled upstairs, muttering about parents who didn't know how to behave in front of their children. Robin and I looked at each other, then retreated to the kitchen. "We're going to have some hot chocolate, okay, Mom?" She didn't answer, so I took that for a "yes."

"Big dinner at Gran's tomorrow," said Robin. "Cousins, uncles, aunts, even David and Karen."

"Mrs. J.'s cooking? Without me?"

"No *she's* not cooking. Everything's being made somewhere else and brought to her house. All she has to do is supervise setting the table and the clean-up. Gran wanted everyone there because it's the last time she'll be in her house at Christmas."

"That's hard on all of you, isn't it?"

He didn't answer for a few seconds. "I love that old house. I have many memories of it. Christmas dinners, birthday dinners, camping out in her backyard, eating fresh carrots from her garden. I caught Dad going all mushy and damp-eyed when he was talking to her on the phone, making plans for moving day. He has even more memories of that place than I do. It's hard on all of us."

I couldn't think of anything to say that would make him feel better, so I took his hand and squeezed it instead.

He tried to smile. "Dad's the only son who lives in town now, but his brothers are both coming home for Christmas this year. My two brothers will be here too, with their squealing kids."

"Where will everyone sit?" I was thinking of the tidy but small dining room.

"That table stretches; it's really quite big when all the bits are pulled out. But they'll probably make me sit at the kid's table in the kitchen with my nieces and nephew to keep the peace. I hate being the youngest uncle in the room; everyone thinks I'm a built-in babysitter."

"Can you escape?" I asked, although I knew the answer to that question even before I asked it.

"I wish. Maybe after dinner; we're eating early because of the three great-grandkids. I'll call you if I can get away."

We stood on the front porch saying goodnight until Andrew stuck his head out his window and yelled "Yuck!" Robin and I both laughed.

"I think that's my signal to leave, Darrah. I'll call you to-morrow."

"Merry Christmas, Robin."

I smiled to myself as I watched his car slowly make its way down the slippery road, the tail lights haloed by falling snow. Once more I tempted the fates by thinking how perfect the day had been, how happy I was.

But nothing happened; Andrew didn't have a seizure on Christmas day, Mom loved the silk scarf I'd bought for her at a small store near Fong's Market, Dad grew silent and almost teary over a picture of the two of us I'd found in one of the photo albums and had scanned, enlarged and framed. In the photo I was about four, wearing a sundress, sitting on a swing; Dad stood behind me, holding on to the ropes of the swing. I had my head tilted up toward him and was smiling; he was looking down at me as if I were the most adorable kid in the world. I don't remember the swing, but it must have been suspended from a tree branch because we were both dappled with leaf shadows.

Andrew was thrilled when he opened my gift and saw the boxed set of *Star Trek Voyager, The Complete Series (Seasons 1–7.)* My new and improved allowance meant that I could get more expensive gifts this year, and I'd enjoyed spending time shopping.

I did well in the gift department, too: a new phone and gift certificates to my favourite stores. I'd begin shopping as soon as the Boxing Day sales started.

Andrew had made me a gift—a shoebox he'd covered with left-over wallpaper from my room, with a package of small file cards inside.

"It's a recipe box," he explained. "Mom helped me make it. It's so you can organize all those recipes you're writing down."

The last gift under the tree was a small flat package wrapped in shiny blue paper. "That's mine," I said, as Andrew picked it up.

"How do you know? It doesn't have your name on it. Maybe it's mine."

"Pass it over. It's from Mrs. J."

It was an old, red book, well used, the insides loosely attached to the cover with yellowing tape. *Foods, Nutrition and Home Management*, Revised 1955.

I ran my fingers over it, almost reverently, as if it were a holy book of some sort.

"That's a crummy gift," said Andrew. "It's old and it's falling apart."

"I think it's wonderful. It's the best present she could have given me."

"If you say so," said Andrew, doubtfully. "Does it have a brownie recipe in it? You still haven't made brownies like you promised you would."

"No, I don't think brownies are in it." I scanned the table of contents. "There's fudge cake, but no brownies. Sorry. But it does have the gingerbread recipe. I'll make some before we go to Aunt Sophie's for Christmas dinner."

"But Darrah, your aunt will have tons of Christmas baking, she always makes too much. We don't need to bring anything else for dessert," Mom protested.

"She won't have gingerbread just like Grandma used to make."

Dad smiled. "No, she won't. But I'd like some, and I'm sure everyone else will as soon they taste it. Go ahead and bake, Darrah, I'll run to the store and pick up some whipping cream."

He gave me a hug on his way out.

Chapter Eighteen

IT WAS THE DAY AFTER Boxing Day, December 27, that I found out. I was in my room, typing up my recipe collection so I could print up cards for my new recipe box, when I thought I heard the doorbell. I didn't pay attention; we'd had a lot of visitors lately—it was the holidays.

"Darrah?" Mom knocked on my closed bedroom door.

"Come in, Mom."

I swivelled my desk chair around, and saw her face. She was pale and had tears in her eyes. She knelt down beside me and looked at me for a long moment before she said anything.

I think I knew what she was going to tell me before she got the words out, but I waited, hoping it wasn't true.

"I'm so sorry, Darrah. It's Mrs. Johnson. She died in her sleep last night."

I bit my lower lip to keep the crying inside, but tears began to push from behind my eyelids anyway. "How . . ."

"Robin's downstairs. He wanted me to tell you first but he wants to see you. He's very upset."

I nodded, still not trusting my voice, and moved past her, almost running down the stairs. Robin stood alone in the living room, his back to the door, looking at the Christmas tree.

"Robin?" I put my hand on his shoulder. He didn't turn around, but a long, shuddering sound came from somewhere deep in his chest.

"Robin, I'm so sorry."

He turned to face me, making no attempt to hide the tears streaming down his face. "She said it was the best Christmas ever, and she was glad everyone was there to spend it with her."

"Robin, I'm . . ."

"I had turkey sandwiches with her yesterday when I brought over the empty boxes she wanted me to get for packing. She . . ."

"It will be okay."

"No, it won't. My grandmother is dead. What's 'okay' about that?"

"Oh, Robin." I held out my arms, and after a few seconds

he came to me, pulled me to him. I felt a tear land on my forehead.

We stayed like that for a while, both of us crying, and then I became aware of people behind us. My whole family stood in the living-room doorway. Andrew was crying, too. "I liked her. I'm sorry, Robin."

"Anything we can do," said my dad, "let us know, okay?"

"Anything," echoed Mom.

Robin cleared his throat and wiped his eyes on his sleeve. "Thanks. Can Darrah and I go over to Gran's? I don't want to go alone, and Mr. Allen asked me to take out the garbage. He was supposed to take it when he left. He had dinner with her last night. But he forgot and he's worried about it smelling."

"I'll get my coat," I said, over my parents' responses.

"Of course, stay as long as you need to, anything we can do, anything . . ."

◆ ◆ ◆

We held hands as we climbed the orange stairs. It had snowed during the night, but ours were not the first footprints on them. The path hadn't been shovelled either. I saw wheel tracks on it, going to the house, then back to the curb. For a moment I visualized a stretcher with a still figure on it being pushed down the path, to the ambulance.

They could at least have brought her out in a pine box, as she wanted, I thought, suddenly angry at the unknown people who had taken Mrs. J. away from her home.

Robin tried to open the door, but it was locked. He climbed back down the stairs, reached underneath the third step, and pulled out a key.

He unlocked the door, we shed our coats and boots and I pulled on the orange slippers. The house was silent. Mrs. J. had never had music or the radio going when I arrived, but somehow I always knew she was there. Now the house felt empty.

"Mr. Allen told Dad she was tired last night. They had soup and toast for supper and she was already in bed when Mr. Allen left."

"I wonder if he knew that would be the last time he'd see her."

Robin stared at me for a long time, before answering. "I wonder. Sometimes people know when these things—when death is near."

I shuddered. "I hope he didn't know. I hope they had a nice supper together, never thinking . . ."

Robin took a deep breath. "The kitchen smells wrong," he said. "But it's not a garbage smell."

I sniffed. "It smells empty. No one is cooking anything." Without thinking, I reached for the flour, the baking powder and a mixing bowl.

"What are you doing?"

"I need to make something for her, for the last time. Then the kitchen will smell as it should and . . ." I burst into tears.

"Let's just grab the garbage and go." Robin took the mixing bowl out of my hands and put it on the counter. "You don't need to cook for her anymore."

"I do, I want to. Baking powder biscuits, she always liked those." I pushed him away and turned the oven on. (General Rules for Soft Doughs, Rule Number One: "See to oven.")

"The whole family, except the little kids, are coming over here this afternoon; Dad and my uncle are trying to decide what to do about a memorial service. Mr. Allen is coming, too. He said she'd left instructions with him, about what she wanted, but I don't know what they are, not yet."

"She had everything organized because she was moving to her new place," I said, remembering how she'd had me write that list. "She knew who she wanted to have her things and made sure it was written down, legally. Mr. Allen has all of that, too."

I found lard in the fridge on the same shelf as it was always kept. "I'll make a double batch of biscuits. Your family will need to have tea and something to eat while they're here."

Robin almost smiled. "Gran always fed us whenever we came to visit. She'd like it, you making biscuits for her family."

As I measured the dry ingredients into the bowl, tiny craters dimpled the flour. For a moment I didn't know what they were, then I grabbed a Kleenex and wiped my eyes. I didn't want to spoil these biscuits, they had to be perfect.

Perfect for her, for Mrs. J.

My voice quavered as I asked, "What did she . . . I mean, was it just old age?"

Robin shook his head. "Cancer."

"Cancer? What do you mean? She was fine except for her broken leg."

Robin shook his head. "No, she wasn't."

"Cancer? She had cancer?"

"We didn't know. She made the doctor promise not to tell us."

I said it again, "Cancer." As if saying the word would make it not true.

Almost without thinking, I had mixed, kneaded and cut out the biscuits. As I put them in the oven and set the timer, I said it again. "Cancer."

"Dad talked to her doctor this morning. The doctor said Gran's cancer was inoperable, and she refused to have chemo-therapy or radiation."

"Why?"

"The doctor told Dad he tried to persuade Gran to go for treatment, but she wouldn't."

"Why?" I asked again.

"How am I supposed to know why? Gran was stubborn."

"You get sick with those treatments," I said. One of Mom's friends died of breast cancer. "You throw up all the time and your hair falls out."

He didn't answer, but started crying again. I did, too. We stood in the middle of the kitchen, arms around each other.

I thought of Mom's friend. She went through months of treatment and then she died anyway. Apparently there was no guarantee that chemotherapy or radiation would work. You might get a little more time before you died—weeks, months—but if you felt terrible and were in pain all time, maybe those treatments weren't worth it.

"Did your father or uncles know?" I asked, my voice muffled in his shoulder.

"No one knew about the cancer except for her doctor, and maybe Mr. Allen and Karen, we aren't sure. The doctor also said that Gran had been in pain for a long time."

"So the pills she took weren't for her leg?"

"No, they were for her cancer pain. But I thought they were for her leg."

"I did, too. How long . . . I mean . . ."

"The doctor said no more than a few months, maybe weeks, but he didn't think it would be this soon. Gran . . ."

I hugged him harder. We stayed like that, clutching each other, crying until the timer dinged.

"Never overcook biscuits," Mrs. J. used to tell me every time I made them. "They'll dry right out, taste like cardboard."

Reluctantly, I left Robin and pulled the baking trays out of the oven. I put the biscuits on racks to cool, and started the dishes. Robin had stopped crying, I could feel him watching me.

"I remember sitting right here, eating gingerbread, watching Gran wash up. She wouldn't eat until she'd washed all the cooking stuff and put everything away."

"A good cook always cleans up after herself," I said, and in spite of myself I smiled, a small smile. "She taught me that."

I covered the biscuits with a clean tea towel, got out the teapot and an assortment of teas and checked to make sure there was enough milk for Robin's family when they came over this afternoon.

At the front door, I pulled off the orange slippers and put them in the basket. Robin took them out again and handed them to me. "Please keep them. You always wear them when you're here. You put them on the day I met you, when I brought you here to help with Gran's tea party. I don't want them donated to a thrift store."

Before I could answer, he was out the door, not looking back. He replaced the spare house key under the third step and called, "See you in the car," his voice rough again. I pulled on my boots and my backpack and had begun to close the front door, when I remembered the garbage. I slipped off my boots again and went back to the kitchen. The bag of garbage wasn't very full. I grabbed it and started to tie it up when I saw what was on top. An empty bottle of Mrs. J.'s pain pills.

"Darrah? Will you bring the garbage? I forgot it," Robin called from the front hall.

This belongs in the recycling, I thought, and slipped the empty pill bottle into my jacket pocket. I'll recycle it at home.

"I've got it, Robin. I'll be right there."

◆ ◆ ◆

Dinner was quiet, no one knew what to say to me. I kept hoping Robin would call, and maybe come over, but I knew he couldn't. He needed to be with his family. Mom and Dad asked me if I wanted to see a grief counsellor. I said I didn't know, maybe.

I went to bed early, exhausted, but I couldn't fall asleep. I couldn't cry anymore, I didn't want to cry anymore. I wanted to sleep. I heard the rest of the family say their goodnights, and Mom came into my room and gently stroked my hair before pulling the covers up and tiptoeing out. I pretended I was asleep, and then tried, again, to really sleep.

Finally, at about two in the morning, I gave up. I took the orange slippers out of my backpack, put them on, and went downstairs. I'd make a cup of chamomile tea; maybe that would help me sleep.

I stood in my own kitchen, waiting for the kettle to boil, looking down at my feet in the orange slippers, and I remembered the pill bottle. It was still in my jacket pocket, hanging in the front hall.

I got it, brought it back to the kitchen, and made a pot of tea. Then I looked carefully at the bottle. It had her name, Mrs. J. Johnson, then the date the prescription had been filled, December 24, and the instructions, "Take one or two every four hours as needed for pain, maximum eight a day." Mrs. J. had died the night of December 26th, or early in the morning on the 27th, the day after Boxing Day, three days after the prescription had been filled. Three times eight is twenty-four.

I looked at the prescription label again. The bottle had held sixty.

I put the bottle on the kitchen table, and poured myself a mug of tea, thinking. That was too many pills for her to take. Maybe she gave some to Mr. Allen? He suffered from arthritis pain. But why didn't she give him the whole bottle? Why take the pills out?

Maybe she got rid of the pills, flushed them down the toilet. Maybe they were in the bottom of the garbage and I hadn't seen them. But why would she do that? She would need more pills the next day and the next. Unless . . .

Unless she took them on purpose.

No. She wouldn't have. Would she? How could she do that? That's not fair to Robin and his family. That's not fair to me.

The tears started again. I gulped down a mouthful of tea. It was hot and burned my mouth. I threw the mug across the room, watched as it shattered against the fridge, almost in slow motion. Chamomile tea dripped down the refrigerator door and onto the floor; part of the broken mug rocked slowly back and forth, slower, slower, and then it stopped. But no one heard the smash; my parents didn't come downstairs to see what was going on.

That's what happens when you die, I thought, still looking at the broken mug. You get slower and slower and then you stop.

Why was I so angry with Mrs. J? She did what she thought was the right thing—the right thing for her. She was strong and brave, but the pain must have been too much. I remembered how at first she just took one pill, then she started asking me for two at a time.

I missed her, I wanted her alive again. I was sad for Robin and sad for me—that I could understand. But why was I angry?

Because it wasn't right. Killing people, even yourself, is wrong.

An image of a circle popped into my mind. Mrs. Barrett was facilitating again, I was sitting beside her, wearing the orange slippers, Robin across the room and Mrs. J. on the other side of Mrs. Barrett. There were others there, Mrs. J.'s family, faceless bodies.

"I will remind you that we are not here to judge Janie Johnson's character," said the imaginary Mrs. Barrett, reading from her imaginary script. "We are here to learn how others have been affected by her actions. Mrs. Johnson, please tell us what you did on that night."

Then the circle vanished. But not before my imaginary Mrs. J. glared at us all and said, "Mind your own business, all of you. Especially you, girl."

It *was* her business, not mine. It was her pain, her suffering, her life. Didn't she have the right to choose to end her own life when and how she wanted? To end the pain? To die with dignity when and where she wanted?

Her family was with her for Christmas, she died in her own home, not in that "warehouse" she had to move to. All good things.

I would miss her, and her family would miss her, but it was her choice.

The prescription label peeled off the bottle easily. I wadded it up into a sticky mass, wrapped it in Kleenex and buried it in the bottom of our almost-full garbage, under crumpled metallic wrapping paper and tangled shiny ribbons. The now unidentifiable empty bottle went back into my jacket pocket, to be tossed into recycling somewhere else, not here where Mom might see it and ask questions.

Then I mopped up the kitchen floor, wiped down the spatters on the fridge and put the broken pieces of the mug in the garbage. I poured out the rest of the tea, put the tea leaves in the compost bucket and rinsed and dried the teapot. Then I hung up the tea towel. The kitchen was tidy again.

"A good cook always cleans up after herself, right Mrs. J?"

Slowly, I climbed the stairs to my bedroom. This time I knew I could sleep.

My Recipes

I made notes and changed some of the words from the General Rules in the Foods, Nutrition and Home Management *book. They were really old fashioned. Also, all of Mrs. J.'s recipes and the ones in her book were in cups and teaspoons, not metric, so I didn't try to change them over. But I looked up some common measurements in metric, and put them on a recipe card. In case I want to make something from a metric cookbook. — DP*

CHANGING MEASUREMENTS TO METRIC:

¼ teaspoon (tsp) = 1.25 ml (milliliter)   ⅓ cup = 75 ml
½ tsp = 2.5 ml   ½ cup = 125 ml
1 tsp = 5 ml   1 cup = 250 ml
1 tablespoon (tbsp) = 15 ml   4 cups = 1 liter
¼ cup = 60 ml

Baking Powder Biscuits

2 cups flour
4 teaspoons baking powder
½ teaspoon salt
2-4 tablespoons fat *(margarine, lard or butter)*
⅔ cup milk or water

- Turn on oven to right temperature (425 degrees for biscuits) and grease baking pans.

- Mix flour and baking powder in a bowl.

- Put shortening in with flour mixture, cut with a knife and work with tips of fingers until mixture is the texture of raw oatmeal *(no big lumps)*.

- Add milk gradually with as little mixing as possible.

- Put dough on a lightly floured board *(or a clean counter)* then knead it. *(Not too long, just until it is all mixed together)*. Roll out until ¾ of an inch thick.

- Cut with floured biscuit cutter *(or a glass the size you want the biscuits to be)*.

- Bake for 15–20 minutes until doubled in size and golden brown on top.

- For cheese biscuits, add ⅔ of a cup of grated cheese to the dry ingredients and reduce the fat to 1 tablespoon.

Barbecued Chicken Rice Soup

1 left-over barbecued takeout chicken *(what remains from the previous meal)*
1 cup of chopped carrots
1 cup of chopped onions
1 cup or more of other vegetables: celery, green peas, beans, red or green peppers, anything you like
½ cup of rice
a bit of oil (small spoonful)
pepper
salt
hot sauce (few drops)

- Pull off as much chicken meat as you can from the left-over chicken; chop and put in a bowl to add later. Put the rest of the chicken (mostly bones) in a big pot of cold water, bring to a boil. Turn the heat down and let it cook slowly, without boiling over, for about an hour.

- Once the stock is ready (it smells good and the bones pull apart easily) remove chicken bones. Let them cool, pull off any more bits of meat you can find and add to the other chicken meat in the bowl. Throw the bones away.

- Chop onion, put in frying pan with teaspoon of oil. Cook for a few minutes until golden coloured, but not burned.

- Add rice, vegetables and chicken to hot stock. Cook for about half an hour until rice is done. Taste, then put in salt, pepper and a few drops of hot sauce if you want it spicy.

Spaghetti Sauce
(Mrs. J. just told me what to do, she didn't have a recipe written down)

1 pound of lean hamburger
1 onion, diced
1 large carrot, peeled and grated
1 tablespoon oregano
1 tablespoon parsley
1 big can of tomato sauce
a few drops of hot sauce
a small bit of black pepper
2 cloves of garlic, peeled and chopped, if you like garlic
Optional vegetables: 2 big mushrooms, washed, diced;
    green or red peppers, diced; black olives, sliced

(You can buy spaghetti sauce already seasoned, called "Italian" or "spiced," or you can add your own seasonings. You don't need to add extra salt, most canned and ready-made foods are already salted quite enough, Mrs. J. says.)

- Brown hamburger in a frying pan until no pink shows. Break it into little chunks while it's browning. Add onion, carrot and garlic—if you are using garlic. Brown for another 10 minutes, making sure it doesn't burn.

- Pour can of tomato sauce into a medium sized saucepan. Add everything from frying pan and oregano and parsley. Carefully bring it to a boil, then turn it down and let it simmer for about half an hour, stirring once in a while.

COOKING THE SPAGHETTI

- Fill the biggest pot you can find ¾ full of water. On high heat, bring it to a bubbling boil. Break dry spaghetti in half first, if you don't like long strings of pasta. Add to boiling water. Watch carefully, turn down heat or it will boil over. Read directions on spaghetti box for how much spaghetti to use and how long to cook it. Don't cook too long or it turns mushy. Pour cooked spaghetti into a colander or strainer over the sink and don't let it get cold.

Wacky Cake

1½ cups white flour
1 cup sugar
1 teaspoon baking soda
1 teaspoon baking powder
3 tablespoons cocoa *(the real cocoa, not hot chocolate mix)*
⅓ cup (or 5 tablespoons) melted shortening , butter or oil
    (margarine is okay, but don't use the diet stuff)
1 tablespoon vinegar
1 tablespoon vanilla
1 cup boiling water

- Put dry ingredients in a 9x9 baking pan *(a square baking pan, not too big)*.
- Make three holes in the mixture. Pour oil, vinegar and vanilla in separate holes.
- Pour boiling water over all. Mix with fork. DO NOT BEAT.
- Bake at 350 degrees for 30 minutes.
- Leave in pan and frost while still warm.

WACKY CAKE FROSTING

½ cup sugar
½ cup milk
2 tablespoons butter
1½ teaspoons flour
½ cup shredded coconut (optional)
½ cup chopped nuts
½ teaspoon vanilla
(I bet ½ cup of chocolate chips would be nice instead of coconut.)

- Combine all ingredients, except vanilla, and cook on medium heat until thick, stir constantly. Add vanilla. Mix well. Spread on warm cake. *(You have to keep stirring or it will stick to the bottom of the pan and burn.)*

Christmas Apple Cider

1 litre apple juice
1 orange unpeeled, washed and quartered or cut in eighths
8 whole cloves (stick one or two into each orange section)
1 whole nutmeg *(it's a round spice that looks a bit like a walnut but you can't break it open, you have to use a grater to get bits off, or use or a sprinkle of ground nutmeg if you don't have the whole nutmegs)*
2 cinnamon sticks

- Put everything in a pot and let simmer for 20 minutes.
- Throw out cinnamon sticks, whole nutmeg and orange pieces and serve hot. *(You can eat the oranges, but be careful of the cloves, they're hard and don't taste that great if you bite into the whole ones.)*

Yule Log

PART 1

1½ cups whole Brazil nuts
1½ cups shelled walnut halves
1 cup pitted dates
1 cup candied peel
½ cup drained green maraschino cherries (whole)
½ cup drained red maraschino cherries (whole)
½ cup seedless raisins

PART 2

¾ cup flour
¾ cup sugar
½ teaspoon baking powder
½ teaspoon salt

PART 3

3 eggs
1 teaspoon vanilla

- Grease sides of bread pan with butter.
- Line with parchment *(baking)* paper.
- Place part 1 in a large bowl. Sift part 2 over part 1, mix well.
- Beat eggs until fluffy. Add vanilla.
- Pour part 3 into parts 1 and 2. Mix well. *(Everyone in the house at the time you make this has to stir the mixture, for good luck.)*
- Bake at 300 degrees for 1½ to 2 hours
- Cool on a wire rack. Don't take paper off.
- When cool, wrap well in foil and keep in the refrigerator.
  (Don't forget to take the baking paper off before you slice it.)

Church Window Cookies

1 cup semi-sweet chocolate chips
¼ cup margarine
3 cups multi-coloured tiny marshmallows
¾ cup chopped nuts

- Melt chocolate and margarine together *(in microwave on low heat, cover and watch it carefully. It should be melted but not too hot).*

- Put in bowl with nuts and marshmallows, stir well.

- On waxed paper *(it can make a mess of the counter if you don't use wax paper)* make dough into "logs" the size you want your cookies.

- Wrap in plastic wrap, then in tinfoil and put in fridge.

- When firm, slice into thin slices and serve.

Fried Rice
(from a recipe on the internet)

1 or 2 green onions
2 large eggs
pepper to taste (a shake or two)
4 tablespoons vegetable oil for stir-frying
4 cups cooked rice
1 to 2 tablespoons light soy sauce or oyster sauce

- Wash and finely chop the green onion —both the white and green parts. Lightly beat the eggs with the pepper. *(You don't need salt, there's lots in the soy sauce.)*

- Heat a wok or frying pan and add 2 tablespoons oil. When the oil is hot, add the eggs. Cook, stirring, until they are lightly scrambled but not too dry. Remove the eggs and clean out the pan.
- Add 2 tablespoons oil. Add the rice. Stir-fry for a few minutes, using chopsticks or a wooden spoon to break it apart. Stir in the soy or oyster sauce. *(Forget the oyster sauce; yuck!)*
- When the rice is heated through, put the scrambled egg back into the pan. Mix thoroughly. Stir in the green onion. Serve hot.

Chinese Stir-Fried Vegetables

1 tbsp vegetable oil
1 slice fresh ginger, chopped into very small bits
2 cloves garlic, minced
¼ cup water
¼ cup soy sauce
1 cup broccoli, chopped
1 green or red pepper, seeded and chopped
½ cup sliced water chestnuts *(they come in a can)*
½ cup fresh bean sprouts *(rinse well and let drain)*
½ cup sliced fresh mushrooms *(rinse and dry with paper towel to get any bits of dirt off before you slice them)*
optional: some chopped bok choy or other Chinese greens *(use mainly the white part with just a bit of the green leafy part)*

- Heat the oil in a large frying pan. *(On medium high heat, not the highest temperature.)* Fry the ginger and garlic for 2 to 3 minutes.
- Carefully add the water, soy sauce and broccoli, fry for 5 to 7 minutes, then add the remaining ingredients.

Hoisin Sauce Chicken Thighs

- Choose some chicken thighs, about two or three for each person.
- Put in a casserole dish, not a deep one, the pieces shouldn't touch.
- Bake at 350 degrees for half an hour.
- Carefully lift out of oven, tilt casserole, spoon out any fat.
- Pour most of the bottle of hoisin sauce *(choose a small bottle)* over the chicken.
- Bake for another half hour.
- Put the extra sauce in a small bowl on the table, in case people want more.

Gingerbread

1½ cup flour
1½ teaspoon baking powder
1 teaspoon ground ginger *(add an extra teaspoon for Mrs. J.s recipe)*
(If you like cinnamon or cloves, you can also add ¼ teaspoon of these to the dry ingredients; it will have a different taste.)
2 tablespoons fat *(Cooking oil or melted butter or margarine, not the diet kind, and you can melt it in the microwave if you watch carefully and just give it 2–3 seconds at a time. Otherwise it boils over and makes a gross mess.)*
1 egg
½ cup molasses warmed
½ cup brown sugar
½ cup milk
Mix according to "Muffin Method"

RULES FOR MUFFIN METHOD
(from Foods, Nutrition and Home Management*)*

- See to oven.
- Prepare pans *(oil or butter them).*
- Measure flour into bowl, add baking soda, sugar and salt, mix with a fork until well mixed. *(The rules actually say, sift together dry ingredients, but I don't sift them, just mix well.)*
- Beat egg.
- Make a depression in flour mixture, then pour in egg, milk and melted fat.
- Stir as little as possible when mixing, then put into well-greased pans.
- Bake in a 350 degree oven for 35 minutes. *(If you stick a toothpick into the middle of the cake or muffin and it comes out clean, not sticky with dough, it's done.)*

DIRECTIONS FOR WHIPPED CREAM

- Put a small carton of whipping cream in the mixer bowl.
- Add two teaspoons of sugar. *(You can add a drop or two of vanilla extract if you want, but not too much.)*
- Beat on low or medium speed *(otherwise it spatters all over)* until cream stays in points *(like tiny mountains)* when you pull the beaters out.
- Put in bowl and serve with chunks of gingerbread. *(Spoon as much cream as you want to on top.)*

ABOUT THE AUTHOR

 Ann Walsh is the author of many books for younger readers including *Your Time, My Time* and *Shabash!* as well as The Barkerville Mystery Series, set during BC's gold rush (*Moses, Me and Murder, The Doctor's Apprentice* and *By the Skin of His Teeth*). She also writes short stories, poetry and creative non-fiction pieces for adults, has compiled and edited three anthologies, and is a facilitator with The Williams Lake Community Council for Restorative Justice. For a complete list of her books, please visit her website at http://ann walsh.ca.